I0527407

Lobster Dreams

A Novel

Stephen Spotte

OPEN
BOOKS

Published by Open Books

Copyright © 2025 by Stephen Spotte

All rights reserved. No part of this book may be reproduced,
scanned, or distributed in any printed or electronic form without
permission except in the case of brief quotations embodied in
critical articles and reviews.

Cover image © Anna Ustymenko shutterstock.com/g/Anna+Ustymenko

Interior design by Siva Ram Maganti

To Jane and John
Thanks for your tolerance

In old times, in the beginning of things, men were as animals and animals as men; how this was, no one knows. But it is told that all were at first men, and as they gave themselves up to this and that desire, and to naught else, they became beasts. But before this came to pass, they could change to one or the other form; yet even as men there was always something which showed what they were.

—Charles G. Leland (1884), *Algonquin Legends*

arthropods ("jointed leg") — invertebrate animals of the zoological phylum Arthropoda (e.g. insects, spiders, crustaceans).

crustaceans ("the shelled ones)" — arthropods of the zoological subphylum Crustacea, mainly aquatic.

decapods ("ten-footed") — crustaceans of the zoological order Decapoda (e.g. barnacles, crabs, crayfishes, lobsters, shrimps).

1.

CAN YOU SING KNOWINGLY of salt and tides, harmonize with whales, suffer a fever though your blood is cold, play mumblety-peg with a razor clam, catch a falling seastar? Since earliest childhood when he developed the capacity to recall dreams his have touched on such fanciful things, but he dreamed while in the guise of a lobster, not a little boy. Even now as a young adult he has never fully experienced the sea, only watched it from the land, intuitively understanding the pitch, roll, and yaw of objects that float on elastic surfaces, and underneath too, a realm of surge, of opaque light and scuttling shadows. In times of cognizance when dream images become unbearably vivid he submerges himself in the tidepool at the base of the hill, feeling the stab of an ancient attachment, a strangely comforting thrill in the susurrous choral voices of restless water.

The land, in contrast, seems only to offer uneasiness and sorrow and the implacable grip and squeeze of gravity. He thinks he ought to somehow remember the sea, although a specific memory never breaks through into consciousness. Each time he eases into the tidepool the sea startles him with its fierce wetness, its ineluctable pressure, the frightening abasement of it scratching

1

against his soul; the demand that he accede to its temporality. And he wonders what, if anything, separates dreams from reality.

When attempting to explain this to Mutha, she says, "Be careful what ye dream, Sonny. Some dreams is more realer than othahs. And anyhow, dreams ain't healthy fah the mind, nah the body. Someday I'll tell ye some stuff, but right now ye're too young fah understandin'." And that's how it stayed: dreams that seemed like real life except experienced in a world under the sea, a place he could only imagine but believed he already knew.

One day Mutha said, "When ye metamorphosed out'n larvahood into a crawlin li'l baby lobstah-like creature, I knowed right off that ye was one o' us — our'n clan, I mean. How it happened that I scooped ye random out'n that tidepool down the hill amongst all them othah larvae was a miracle o' luck, I reckon. Me biological clock wahnt jist tickin along quiet-like, it had put the hammah down, and I was hopin' to be a mutha and give it the ol' hot suppah. I was keenin' fah a young-un to mutha, nevah thinkin that out'n the millions o' larvae driftin' in the ocean I'd chance to seine up one o' me own. On hatchin' ye was tiny as a mosquito. Ye rose to the suhface and ye'd a'bin swimmin' free fah three weeks. And as ye growed ye begun lookin' like our'n kin and gainin' the same troubles o' our'n. But I still seen ye as a blessin'.

"Ye was raised in that li'l aquarium in the conah yondah. Each mornin' I crept down the hill to the tidepool and drub up two buckets o' fresh seawatah to change it out so's ye wouldn't die swallerin' the poison o' ye own excrements. And I pulled a plankton net through the same pool at low tide and caught zooplankton, which I emptied into the buckets and totin' 'em back up the hill so's ye'd have somethin' nutritious to eat. Ah, what a cunnin' bit o' larva ye was, practically transparent 'cept' fah them big black buggy eyes. But ye're growed now, finished school, and I reckon ye'll be leavin' soon. Time's a'gainin' on me, and we need to have us a confab. Reach me the octofocals. These ol' compound eyes is gettin' wusah by the day." She adds, "And hand 'em ovah careful. Gotta membah this lobstah-claw syndrome o' our'n, which tain't improvin' fah us neithah one. It's a bitch pickin' up stuff without ye hardly got fingahs. And walkin' is a bummah too when ye got jist a pointy toe on all ye walkin' feet. But I need to tell ye some things 'cause I reckon ye'll be leavin' soon."

Her words and their tone startle him. "You've said it twice now Mutha, that I'll be leaving soon. Why?"

"'Cause it's time ye went out inna wuld and found ye place. I'm a'sendin' ye to the coast Downeast to ye uncle. He's ovah to Suramoh Island neah the spot me and 'im was raised up. Now, go on and draw me a bahth o' cold seawatah. I'll need to get off'n me pins and float a spell aftah the confab. Gravity's done drove all me joints to weak-kneed oblivion. They ache somethin' awful, and I'm stove up."

He half-crawls, half-stumbles to the bathroom and the old porcelain-covered iron tub with its lion-foot legs and turns on the pump. Frigid seawater directly from the Gulf of Maine pours from the spigot. The inline thermometer registers sixty-two degrees Fahrenheit, just to Mutha's liking.

He shuts off the water and returns slowly and with great effort to the living room. "But what will I do on Suramoh Island? I've never been there. I've never heard of it, and I've never met Uncle. I don't even know what he looks like. Do you have a picture of him?"

"No pitchah, but he looks a good deal like us, and I figgah ye and 'im kin decide what to do. I've barely met 'im meself. He sent me a buthday cahd once, but it was his buthday, not mine. Anyhow, ye turned out a piss-poah chicken fahmah, no aptitude a'tall. Instead, ye went and got educated at that there Downeast Univusity, which tain't even all the way Downeast, and they taught ye to talk propah, like them summah tourist folk who come-from-a'ways, takin' pitchahs and eaten' lobstah. I cahnt see why ye should stick around heah. Git out and make ye place in the wuld. I'll miss ye some when ye're gone, but it's fah the best." A couple of drops of salty water drip down her face. She sniffles and tries to furrow her brow, but it seems to be stuck. "I ain't so good at fahmin' chickens meself, bein' honest with ye. I thought I'd be keepin' chickens o' the sea like I seen advahtised on the teevee. Ye know, Charlie the Tuna. Or mebbe I'd be a'growin' out baby lobstahs to legal-size chicken lobstahs, chix the lobstahmen calls 'em. Then heah come the stock and it wahnt neithah. The damn things is feathahed, ain't a'one o' 'em got webbed feet, and they cahnt swim fah spit, all of 'em sinkahs."

She tries shaking her head but her neck and body are fused. She holds up her deformed lobster-claw hands, a congenital malady that afflicts them both. "Goddam-mah!" she says with anguish, segueing into an epenthesis, "and this heah authah-ite-us in evah last leg joint, cahnt hahdly walk a step a'fah takin' a diggah flat on me snout. Ayuh, it aches wicked bad, and I got me a painful crick in the uppah carapace. Sonofabitch don't swivel. Now, if'n ye got any questions a'fah me bahth, ast 'em."

"Okay, why am I called Sonny? Is it a family name?"

"Yea and doh. All lobstahs o' the male kind is called

Sonny when they gain stage foah o' metamo'phosis and molt into actual li'l lobstahs that crawls on the bottom like the growed-uns. It's easiah that a'way, givin all o' ye the same name, 'specially 'cause baby lobstahs looks alike. Was ye female instead ye'd a'bin called Missy. Same with all family names: Uncle, Auntie, Mutha, Fatha, Hoosbin, Wife, Coosin. . .ye get the idea. Family stuff, I s'pose. Basically, in lobstah society ye're named accordin' to the rung o' the ladder ye're stand' on. Anythin' else? I could use me a good long soak."

"What about my brothers and sisters, and who's my father?"

"I'll tackle the second question fust. Truth be told, who the hell knows? The old sayin' that it's a wise young lobstah what knows its fatha is true. Same in reverse fah wise old fatha lobstahs, so ye ain't likely to find out. Now, aboot the fust question, us females sheds eggs evah two yeahs, meanin' the same as sayin evah othah yeah, beginnin' at the ages o' three to eight, actual age dependin' on watah temp'ature and such. The ones livin' in wahm watah ages quickah. But figgah age five when a lady lobstah on 'er fust spin around the dance floah holds between five thousand to thuty-six thousand eggs. A lobstah ten inches long lays around ten thousand eggs. A big female, say, o' sixteen inches and aboot eighteen yeahs, kin hold a hunnert-thousand eggs. That was me in me prime.

"And a berried lady in such condition — that's one carryin' developin' embryos, I s'pose 'cause they look like tiny berries, black and all — totes 'er brood fah nine months mebbe, same as a human woman. I had the widest abdomen in the whole Gulf of Maine. It could hold developin' embryos by the hunnert-thousands, and when I wiggled me tail fans in the faces o' them males while squeezin' out a few hits o' pheromonal pahfume they went bonkahs. They'd go to sniffin' in that likable smelly-smell and dancin' aboot like idiots, all to git me close fah try'na sneak 'tween me swimmerets, the hahny buggahs.

"Yep, as I was sayin', at the end o' me time down below I was a fifteen poundah. The lobstahs that come off the land to watah knowed me as Big Mutha. Them was the fahmahlies, as they still call 'em. It means they was fahmahly humans but now is lobstahs who somehow kin still talk to one anothah like nahmal Mainah humans 'cept fah lackin' a human mouth, voice box, lungs, and a brain. Nobody evah figgahed how they manage it, 'cept they sure as hell do.

"Jeezum crowbah! I cahnt recall how many times I been berried, so don't 'spect me to membah each o' the li'l buggahs I lugged undah me abdomen squoze asshole to elbow and cemented to me swimmerets. In case ye forgot, the swimmerets is them leetle paddlin' thingies hangin' undah ye abdomen fah stickin' embryos on and fah movin' watah 'tween ye legs. And ye think I membah the names o' the fathas that went and caused me pre-dicament? I'm tellin' ye, they was all jist called Hoosbin, and coulda been more'n one per brood, but only one fatha at a time." She waggled a no-no with what might have been a pointer finger were it not so misshapen and hard. "Nope, jist one customah at a time fah us ladies. Some calls it serial monogamy, othahs say it's skankin' around. Think in ye imagination o' dancin' and switchin' pahtnahs when the music stops.

"Sometimes me and a hoosbin done the wiggle agin in his sheltah while me shell was firmin' up aftah a molt, and sometimes I left 'im and moved into anothah hoosbin's sheltah. If'n this is confusin' it means a brood might have more'n one fatha. It's a big hahny ocean. But names? All hoosbins looks alike when the light's off, I'm tellin' ye. I kin tell ye this too: the only guaran-damn-tee a hoosbin has o' bein' the one and only fatha is when 'im and the wife does the benthic boogie jist aftah she molts, and she does it only with 'im 'til the offspring is sprung. Why? 'Cause any sperm she's a'holdin' and savin' inside to fertilize 'er eggs ovah the comin' months is discah-ded along with 'er shell if'n she ups and molts agin a'fah extrudin' and fertilizin' them eggs. And if this ain't clear neithah, it means a hoosbin who done impregnated that wife, 'im all giddy and dumb as a cold lobstah gnudi, is shit out'n luck and won't be propagatin' his line if'n she then goes and molts. But none o' that's the fault o' us muthas, who jist hauls the load, and if it wahnt fah fierce infant mortality o' them larvae they be stacked atop the Gulf o' Maine high as the ass on a tall giraffe."

He frets the night through, feeling unprepared and unformed. He didn't have his shit together, his feces col-lated, his excrement compiled, and now he would be on his own for the first time. The next day Mutha and he rouse old Dobbin and hitch him to their only other piece of rolling stock, a decrepit wooden cart balanced on a junkyard axle with a cracked automobile tire at each end. Into it they load a case of motor oil and a punch-style motor oil dispenser, several carboys of gasoline, some food, and a change of overalls. They don't own much. He's sad to be leaving, but Mutha doesn't appear to be taking his departure too hard and seems almost cheerful.

"I'm sorry to see ye go, and Dobbin too, but ye both needs to git out'n the wuld. Not too hahd as I thought pushin' Dobbin out'n the bahn, the place he's bedded all 'is life. Mebbe he's a'lookin kindly to ye trip Downeast, ayuh. Take it slow, them tahrs ain't got much gription left. Chout fah cahs and the Massholes drivin' 'em, it bein' the tourist season, I'm tellin' ye."

"How will I find Uncle?" He was still nervous about this undertaking.

"When ye gets to the village I named, go to the dock and gob 'round with them ne'er-do-wells. Uncle comes to the mainland evah so often fah supplies — bait and such — and ast anybody which lobstahman is Uncle and which boat tied at the dock be 'is'n. They'll tell ye. Fishin' folk is nosy. Might have to sleep in the caht a night, mebbe two, but taint likely ye'll miss seein' 'im eventually. We packed ye enough salt mackerel to hunkah down a spell. Tell the bunch o' derelicts lollygaggin' at the dock that Nephew is a'seekin' Uncle, and he'll come find ye when he hits the mainland. I'm shooah he's out straight this tourist season, catchin' lobstahs fast as he kin. Them come-from-a'ways, they be lined up at the lobstah shacks a'waitin' on lobstah dinnahs with cahn' on the cob and steemahs, ayuh. Well, 'nough lip-flappin. Bye, the two o' ye."

With these words she turns and limps away, leaving Sonny and Dobbin adrift in a new life.

2.

THEY DRIFT AND RATTLE onto the shoulder, Dobbin
huffing and wheezing as if on his last struts, the trailer
jolting painfully through roadside ruts that cause its contents to shift and rattle alarmingly. Billows of unpleasant
brown dust trail behind and roil up from underneath the
wheels like a blast of earthy halitosis. A curious farmer
watches from his pasture as this pitiful, barely articulated
congeries lurches to a stop.

When the disturbance abates, the farmer speaks.
"Ah," he says. "Ayuh." He has come closer and is leaning
on the top rail of a split-rail fence, attired in farmer johns
that in better days had been blue-and-white striped. A
straw hat covers most of his face and renders his eyes
invisible. He has one foot propped on a lower rail and
the other anchored to the ground. Then he shifts legs.
"Bet ye cahnt do that," he says with a sneer.

"Do what?" said Sonny

"Move ye feet thisaway." He shifts his feet back to
their original positions.

"No," Sonny says truthfully. "I don't have good
balance."

"Not suhprised. Ye sort nevah does. Clumsy as the
devil," the farmer speaks these words not unkindly.

"Ye come-from-a'ways in that contraption? What's ye up home?"

"Three nights on the road." Sonny names the coastal village near where he and his mother lived. The farmer looks at the heavens and squints as if seeking inspiration from a cloud. "Yup, that'll aboot do 'er. Nine mile south o' heah as the vulture flies. If'n I got me 'rithmetic right that's three mile a day. Seems slow even fah ye sort. Woulda been fastah by sea, ayuh, I'm tellin' ye. I reckon ye're now headed uppayondah back to the coast takin' the long-aboot way, ayuh.

"Hah!" the farmer says suddenly. He grips the fence rail with both hands and leans back suddenly like an accelerating water skier. "Ye're one o' them, ain't ye." It was a statement.

"One of what?"

"Them wingnut come-from-a'ways with bony legs and knobby knees. I see 'em pokin out'n ye pant legs, mebbe half a dozen of 'em. It's why ye cahnt walk propah, all woody and wobbly. And lookie them hands hid inside mittens, fah shooah. Makes 'em seem like paws, it does, claws most likely. Some folk in these pahts — the nah-mal folk — claims to o' seen ye kind walkin the back roads undah dahk o' night actin like ye're lookin fah food. Betcha ye use them hands like spatulas fah scoopin up roadkill to take home and cook, heh, heh." He makes scooping motions. "And ye feet: betcha if'n ye was to takin' off'n ye boots ye'd have jist one pointy toe on 'em each, ayuh." He pulls a grass stalk from the bodacious space between his front teeth and licks it some. He says, "I see ye got a wee stumble to ye stride, heh, heh. Ayuh, I betcha ye be one o' them."

Sonny cringes. It's true about his hands: he's missing

the index, middle, and ring fingers; the thumbs and opposing pinkies curve grotesquely inward giving the hands a claw-like appearance. Naturally, this had made him laughable in grammar school when students were learning to write in cursive. His penmanship was always a topic of amusement, judged worse in class by peers and teachers alike. Sonny thinks, he's got me there. And his legs? Not much to add except that he will never *ever* pull on a pair of shorts, preferring death by torture. Still, he's curious about the farmer's "your kind" comment and what it might signify, so he says, "What do you mean by 'one of them?'"

"Hahd tellin' not knowin'. Them historicals, I s'pose, what come-from-a'ways, humdingahs all. Been amongst us nahmal folk fahevah, seems like, ayuh. Nobody knows whar they come from, doh, they don't." He shakes his head. "Some says the land, some the sea. But whatevah, they be shamblin' and limpin' awful, the lot, same like ye're doin', and havin' hands the same. They got only a scrid o' sense, and bein' dubbahs they cahnt fahm fah spit."

Sonny says, "I got lost, that's all, and Dobbin here is tired." He bends forward and extends a carapacial pat. It's all he can manage before succumbing to gravity, which is yanking at him from down below, there on the ground. With an abrupt lurch he falls off the seat and collapses onto his ventrum, each leg of his overalls stuffed with four appendages. He's twitching fearfully and doesn't give a good goddamn who might have been watching. The only possible witness is the farmer, at that instant focusing on Dobbin and failing to notice his pratfall followed by the humbling squabble of crunching sounds emanating from his overalls, like cornflakes belabored under shoe leather.

"Ayuh. He's hot and thusty," says the farmer, "and plum wore down, sad ol' fellah. And I betcha he's low, awful low."

"How low you figure?" Sonny manages to say from his prone position, face stuck in the form-fitted dirt.

"Hahd tellin' not knowin'. Mebbe one, mebbe two, but could be moah, could be less. Cahnt say fah suhtun till I check the stick."

"The stick."

"Ayuh chummy, the stick."

The farmer steps over the fence and approaches. He twists and bends until in position to examine Dobbin in frontal view, whereupon he proclaims, "One eye glassy and tahd-lookin', one eye missin'." He puts the back of his hand gently against Dobbin's brow while gazing thoughtfully into the distance. "Ovahheated too, ayuh. I'll fetch the watah. Back in a jiff. Don't run off, heah?" He chuckles knowingly.

He returns with a watering can and lifts the top of Dobbin's carapace, gingerly removing a threaded piece of the innards while protecting his hand with a rag. Steam rolls out the opening. When the flow subsides he sticks the spout of the can into the hole and empties it. "Almost bone dry," he says. Next, he pulls out the dipstick. "Ayuh, down a coupla quahts, as I figgahed." He rummages in the cart finding the motor oil and oil dispensing tool. He punctures two cans, empties their contents into the crankcase, and wipes his hands on the chest of his overalls. Satisfied, he grunts, steps back over the fence, and resumes leaning with arms crossed on the top rail as if expecting the scene to repeat. From there he squints at his handiwork through the ten feet of distance, one patty-hoppered foot planted on the ground, the other raised and resting on the bottom rail. Suddenly, he shifts his feet and reverses their position. "Betcha ye cahnt do that," he says with a grin.

"Do what?"

"This." He rapidly returns his feet to their original positions. "Ye'd fall on ye arse fah shooah. I reckon what passes fah ye arse, ayuh."

"You showed me that trick before." Sonny manages to bend his wrists downward and push himself upright onto the tips of his fingers. With considerable effort he totters upright, feeling shamed and abased, flooded by the memory of adolescent taunts in that fishing village where he grew up. Nautical terms were part of the lexicon, and when he tumbled in the schoolyard and struggled to stand his classmates would shout, "Ahoy, ahoy, Lobstah-Buoy!"

The farmer watches dispassionately, making no move to assist. "As I figgahed. Ye're one o' them. Be ye gone now. I done me Christian duty to help ye, though I bet Christ hisself never seen ye like. So, keep goin' on ahead till ye comes to the coast or bang ye a uey and head back to come-from-a'ways whar ye was, tain't no diff'rence to me, ayuh. I'm out straight and got hay to fok fah me cows." With that, he turns and without looking back walks toward the other side of the pasture.

3.

"THIS HEAH'S ME ASSISTANT, Homarus, but we calls 'im Homah. He's also me nephew, makin' 'im ye coosin." Homer is egg-shaped with short rickety appendages that bend all whichy ways. He appears to be lacking a neck, and his bald undersize head seems to have been stuck haphazardly atop his torso as an afterthought, a failed attempt at symmetry.

Uncle steps back and looks at Homer fondly. "He's a genius in his own way, Homah is. Why, the pinchahs on his second and thud walkin' legs is like socket wrenches, seems they was bahn to tighten and loosen hex nuts on machinery. And he's ambidextrous, both sides bein' equal good."

He turns to Sonny. "So, what I think we should do is teach ye the lobstah trade. This is how she wuks. I own me own boat, the *Sucatsa*. I'm 'er captain and drivah. Ye coosin Homah heah is the sternman. He handles the dock lines and the anchorin' and pullin' and baitin' the traps we sometimes calls pots. When we come up on one o' me pot buoys I put *Sucatsa* to idle. Homah heah, he takes the buoy hook — that's a pole with a hook at the end — and he hooks the line jist behind the buoy to pull 'er close so's he kin stick the line in the winch hook,

14

which he's a'holden' in 'is othah hand, to pull up the pot. I like fishin' singles and got jist one trap to a buoy. Aftah the winch hook has got gription on the pot line, Homah kicks on the winch and lifts that pot out'n the watah and pulls 'er on deck. If'n it's jist 'im and me and the sea tain't too rough, I leave the wheel and go hep out, 'specially if'n the catch is a big-un.

"We take the lobstahs out'n the trap and chuck the shahts ovah the side. Shahts is what we calls the undahsize ones that tain't legal to keep. We band the claws o' the keepahs, closin' 'em tight with rubbah bands so's the buggahs cahnt fight and injah one anothah, and pitch 'em in the livewell. Damaged lobstahs is wuth less at the dock than healthy ones. Them with one claw is the culls. We keep 'em if'n they be legal size, but they ain't wuth much. The come-from-a'ways don't like seein' a one-handed lobstah on the dinnah plate. Homah, he rebaits the pot and draps it ovah the side, but sometimes he keeps it on deck if'n I decide to dite it someplace else, what we hope is a wicked pissah fishin' spot.

"Aftah a day on the watah a'checkin' and rebaitin' pots we come home to weigh and log in the catch and add our lobstahs to the pound, which is the big floatin' pen down to the dock fah holdin' the community's catch o' live lobstahs 'til the trucks take 'em to come-from-a'ways places like Baston and New Yawk. Aftah ye get the job down pat it'll be a tetch bettah fah me and Homah, havin' the extry sternman. And ye kin live with me and 'im. Got plenty o' room up to the house."

Sonny thanks Uncle and says, "The name of your boat, *Sucatsa*, is it Maine Native American? Maybe Wabanaki or Algonquin?"

"Naw, it's jist that *Sucatsa* is *Astacus* spelt backwuds.

One o' the state fish and game fellahs told me that *Asta-cus* was the fust scientific name give to the lobstah, so I named me boat *Sucatsa* to mess with them smahty-pants come-from-a'ways. And ye might o' noticed that the name Suramoh Island is Homarus spelt backwuds. *Homarus* is the lobstah's second scientific name and Homah's namesake. Cahnt say who come up with that idea o' namin' the island, but wahnt me." He gives a sort of chuckle.

Sonny has another question: "Mutha says we're kin, so how do we know we aren't catching and selling our relatives to become lobster dinners?"

Uncle takes off his Greek fisherman's cap and scratches the point of his head. "That's a good question, fah shooah. Best I kin tell ye is, it don't make a nevah-mind wuth spit, considerin' that lobstahs eat anythin', includin' othah lobstahs. I got to admit that me and Homah, we enjoy a nice lobstah dinnah now and agin, but we only eat the culls, 'cause the boat price — that's what they pays us fah our catch at the dock — tain't wuth much, as I bin sayin'. Well, I got to go 'range to git Dob-bin and ye caht ovah to Suramoh."

4.

Dawn on Sonny's first work day. He, Uncle, and Homer are loading *Sucatsa* with bait. Uncle says to Sonny, "Have ye notice that big yellah lobstah in the aquarium yondah?" He nods in its direction. Sonny says he has, and in fact had stared closely at it for several minutes. "Me and Homah calls 'im Sonny 'cause he looks like kin. Got to look close, then ye see the family likeness."

"Sonny is my name too," Sonny says.

"I believe it is," says Uncle. "But I betcha Mutha told ye that all young male lobstahs is called that. This heah lobstah is special 'cause he's what they call a golden lobstah. A fellah from the Downeast college, a puhfessah he said he was, come by the dock one day. Crippled gent with jist one leg and one ahm and hobblin' on a crutch. He tells us a lobstah like this is wicked hahd to find, one in aboot thuty million, makin' 'im extry special. We keep 'im in this big glass box with runnin' seawatah fah the come-from-a'ways to goggle at. Mostly they talk aboot how he'd taste with lemon and melted buttah. But he ain't a legal keepah. Bein' so big, the law says he's a breedah and needs to go back to the ocean. I caught 'im, so I'm responsible fah releasin' im. We'll do that in the fall when the come-from-a'ways leave. Them's the tourist folk, most of 'em Massholes from Massachusetts."

"What's that sign underneath the aquarium say?"

"Hahd tellin' not knowin'. It's wrote by furrinahs. That same puhfessah gent brung it one day. Couple o' students was a'totin' it fah 'im 'cause he's crippled and all. He ast us to nail it undah the stand holdin' up the aquarium, so some o' the dock rats — that's the men not havin' jobs and jist hangin' out at the lobstah pound smokin' and laughin' and passin' the bottle and tellin' lies — they went and fetched a hammah and some nails and done it. The puhfessah told us it's a sayin' by some famous egghead."

And so, over the remainder of that spring and through the summer Sonny was a lobsterman, and he and his crewmates came to compose an efficient team despite their severe handicaps. Uncle had been right: three were indeed better than two, and Sonny caught on quickly. He learned how to measure lobsters, deciding which were keepers and went into the livewell and which were shorts that went back to the sea. He and Homer took turns operating the winch, and they pulled traps aboard together, after some practice coordinating their efforts like a pair of disciplined dancers. And Uncle even let him run the boat on several occasions when they were well at sea and not near any rocks or buoys. He was enjoying the work and liked having been accepted into the close community of lobster fishers. For the first time he had the feeling of belonging. Not only had he become self-supporting, but he was contributing to the livelihood of a larger group. In a few words, he was happy and satisfied.

That first summer ends with the crew having earned a tidy profit. The maples and birches are changing into their autumn colors, the air is turning chilly, and the come-from-a'ways have gone. The Maine coast is quietly awaiting winter and closing of the lobster fishery for another season. Traps have been pulled and stored, and the crew will spend its time until spring beside the potbelly stove in Uncle's work shed repairing damaged traps and making new ones. They will string replacement potlines, marking the buoys for identification with the number of Uncle's state lobstering license. *Sucatsa* will soon go into drydock where her crew will scrape and paint her hull, and Homer has been as planning the annual engine overhaul. However, they still must make a last trip to sea to release the big yellow lobster.

The morning starts nasty and worsens. Although the sun shines brightly as they embark, a blustery onshore wind rips away the tops of the waves, transplanting the spray to their faces. The idea is to head to the general location where the lobster had been caught and release him near his home grounds, then return to the dock for coffee and donuts to celebrate the season's end with confrères and family.

They find the release site using the GPS. Uncle swings the bow north, bringing *Sucatsa* parallel to the steepening swells. The wind, now gusting wildly from the east, is hammering their starboard side causing *Sucatsa* to pitch and yaw and generally wallow in some distress over her mutability. There's no need to anchor. Uncle shouts to Homer and Sonny to drop the lobster off the port side. Sonny removes it from the live well and clutches it to his chest while Homer, to steady them both, grips the back of Sonny's oilskin jacket. Both stumble when *Sucatsa* dips sideways into a deep trough. Homer loses his hold as Sonny leans over the gunnel in preparation to let go of the lobster. Sonny and the lobster pitch into the sea.

Sonny feels his sensorium flip upside-down, also sideways, in-and-out, ass-over-teacup, and all-to-hell-and-gone; in other words, his world has become a different world, and not just transitioned from air to water, which god knows aren't identical, but Sonny himself has experienced a change too. He is now someone (or something) else and about to realize he's metamorphosed into a lobster. During the pendency of that transition, shorter than the blink of an eye, he has become fully crustaceanized. No longer a freak with lobsterish traits, he now is a true one-hundred-percent lobster. Except, as he is to learn, one that retains the capacity to think as a human and converse telepathically with rare others of his kind, known among themselves as formerlies (for formerly human). He later recalls Mutha having mentioned them.

From this new vantage he sees Uncle leaning over the gunnel submerged past where his neck should be and still wearing his Greek sailor cap. He seems to be shouting as his blurry image rises and falls with the swells. Bubbles emerge from his mouth along with buzzing sounds like *hummm* and *humm* and even *hummmmm*. But his words are clear, if only in Sonny's head. What he says is, "Ye won't be suhfacin' 'cause ye're now a lobstah. We won't be looking' fah ye. Wouldn't do no good, and folks back home will undahstand. Tail-flip on away from heah, Nephew! Git down out'n the watah column! Might be a big mutha cod waitin' to swallah ye like a bit o' lobstah bait! Head fah the bottom and find ye a nice safe crevice amongst the rocks. And keep ye powdah dry!" With that, he gives a sodden wave and disappears above the roiling surface.

5.

SONNY DRIFTS DOWNWARD, SPINNING slowly with legs flailing, instinctively seeking the solid substrate. He's unbalanced, uncertain how to right himself in this place where up and down seem the same. Shadows flicker all around, unjamming and firing his proprioception systems into action as he back-flips desperately toward the dimness below. Once on the bottom he realizes that the shadows he's feared are merely shifting bands of light reflecting off the seafloor.

He looks up. The depth is shallow, not more than three fathoms, and the broken surface overhead is fracturing the downwelling light into these ripples known as caustics, their contrast with the background spacelight in the horizontal distance is enhanced slightly by his polarized vision. He fails to notice the reason, unaware of having suddenly acquired this sensory feature. Nor does he actually know what caustics are. He's in the dark about oceanography, out of his league and a bunch of other platitudes. Come to think of it, on the subject of oceanography he doesn't know jack-shit.

His vision, awful on land, is no better underwater. At the moment he can perceive light and movement, but bringing even nearby objects into focus is dodgy. The temperature on the deck of Uncle's lobster boat had felt chilly, but down here is comfortable. He knows that at this time of year the sea is often warmer than the air, and on this morning the Gulf of Maine feels downright cozy.

Everything else is strange too, especially what feels like the greater density and tighter elasticity of the medium in which he is now immersed, which actually is about the same density as his tissues, and although he can't swim neither has he been flattened to the ground, as so often was the case on becoming too exhausted on land to support his own weight. Until now, wallowing in the tidepool was the closest he's come to being immersed in the ocean. For the first time he's completely submerged. Can he swim? Probably not. The tail-flipping episode only propelled him a short distance backward with little directional control on his part. Not real swimming. Actually, he's now able to move forward along the bottom with a bouncy sort of buoyancy. He takes several hesitant steps, legs moving out of synchrony like those of a knackered horse. However, in just minutes his newly wired autonomic nervous system brings the muscles and tendons into proper alignment. Million years of continuing evolution have not been derailed by these puny difficulties.

The organs and cells by which a lobster senses and interprets the world are not easily identified, except vision, which features the obviously prominent eyes. Specific structures for the rest — hearing, touch, taste, and smell — rarely are obvious, either not clustered and centrally located or multi-modal, sharing and often mutually obscuring other sensory functions. To Sonny, the ramifications are soon apparent.

On reaching the bottom Sonny is immediately aware

that his auditory world has changed. There seems to be no noise from the engine of Uncle's boat idling overhead, yet he feels its vibrations. Does this mean there's no sound, or there is and he's gone deaf? Not exactly. There indeed is sound, and whether he's deaf depends arguably on how hearing is defined. He tries lifting his lobster-claw hands to feel his ears, finding they have been transformed into even clumsier real lobster claws. He tentatively raises his first two pairs of walking legs, slender and flexible and terminating in tiny pincers and gently touches the two places near the front of his body where ears should be, feeling only smooth surfaces. Nothing like an ear protrudes on either side. Not surprising because he no longer has a distinctly separate head. It's become fused with his body.

The boat's engine, source of the sound, continues generating a series of pressure waves traveling steadily outward. Simultaneously, these waves are causing water molecules they encounter (think of them as individual "particles") to oscillate in place — that is, to vibrate. Envision these "particles" transmitting the energy of their motion to adjacent particles, in turn displacing them from their present stationary positions and inducing them to oscillate. Unlike a pressure wave that travels outward from a source, oscillating particles do not change location, they shimmy and shake in place. Sonny *feels* the engine's sound — the vibrations it generates — through specialized organs in his legs, antennules (the short, bifurcated first antennae), second antennae (the two long "feeler" antennae), claws, and mandibles (crustacean "jaws") — but can't *hear* it; in other words, he's incapable of detecting the pressure component of sound, generally considered commensurate with hearing. To answer Sonny's question, he's now deaf by one definition, although perhaps not according to another. Nonetheless, he surely can't "hear" as he once did. If indeed there could be music under the sea, Sonny will never know whether it's sensitive and harmonic or querulous and dissonant. He will perceive only its vibrations.

Deaf or not, lobsters aren't entirely mute. They produce buzzing sounds by the rapid contraction of muscles at the base of the second antennae causing the carapace to vibrate. Lobsters are among the few crustaceans that generate sounds internally, although their putative functions are largely conjectural. Communication with other lobsters has been suggested, but not demonstrated. Buzzing has been correlated with stress, reported during male-male agonism (aggression between members of the same species), and when piscine predators are nearby.

Many other surprises await, but these are momentarily subsumed in a more pressing matter: finding a safe place to hide. The sun is still high, and Sonny feels vulnerable in the open. He's dimly aware of having shrunk considerably from his human size, probably by fifteen times or more. Having become considerably smaller, everything now seems larger. Time to get busy and look for a suitable shelter, instinct dictating its ideal specifications to be dim, low-profile, height about one-half the width.

Uncle's traps have been set on rocky bottom, a site selected for its lobster-friendly terrain, meaning it's a good location for finding both food and shelter. In short order Sonny locates a crevice under a rock suitable at least temporarily. It has a lumpy ceiling populated by sessile organisms of various sorts, plant and animal. It has a sandy floor. Not a room such as he is used to, although it might provide safety, but from what? Predators, he supposes, and maybe marauding male lobsters intent on evicting him and moving in. These big claws he's now examining are probably useful for purposes other than cracking clam shells. Not bad for a starter shelter, except for the flooding issue, he thinks sardonically. From now on the wet is normal, the dry to be avoided; it's the dry that could suffocate him.

This room is cold and damp, you say? What else can be expected at the bottom of the ocean? No, it doesn't have a bathroom, kitchen, or laundry facilities. Meh. Superfluous amenities after becoming a benthic predator-scavenger. Without prompting, his second antennae — again, the longer "feelers" of the two pairs of antennae he's been given — sweep over his new home, lightly touching their surfaces and receiving the haptic responses reassuring him of its adequate dimensions. Interesting tools, these antennae. He curls his abdomen and backs up until hitting solid rock. So, the crevice has a sloping ceiling tapering inward. It has irregular walls of rough granite providing tight security on three sides, everywhere except the entrance.

Once ensconced Sonny's main activities will consist of keeping house and personal grooming. The house-keeping chore, assuming he sticks around at least several days, will be periodically ridding the shelter of debris that drifts in and broken shells and other leftovers from meals collected during foraging and brought home to eat in comfort and safety. Lacking a rug under which to sweep this clutter, Sonny will instead put the tips of his claws together and push the stuff bulldozer-style out the door. When not away foraging he will then spend the remaining idle time at home grooming himself. This consists of haptically examining every part of his body using the tiny pinchers of the first two pairs of walking legs and methodically scissoring away or pulling off newly settled epibionts such as algae, barnacles, and other sessile organisms seeking to attach permanently to his body. Only a small patch on a lobster is unreachable. This is the areola, a place on the dorsal surface of the carapace between where shoulder blades are located in humans. There, as a result of serendipitous placement during larval settlement, flourishes a mixed colony of epibionts, safe until the lobster's next molt when these uninvited hitchhikers will be discarded with the shell.

6.

THE REST OF THE day and that first night pass in a state
of high alert. He realizes intuitively that his circadian
cycle needs reversing: he must hide and rest during the
day and venture out to forage at night. In addition, he
has not yet had time to learn which signals from the environment convey important information about sources of
food and danger and which are simply irrelevant com-
ponents of the background. Reversing and resetting his
circadian clock will influence his motor functions and
also improve his eyesight: visual sensitivity is enhanced
during the crepuscular hours of dawn and dusk and at
night, periods when lobsters are most active.

He has become increasingly sensitive to subtle
changes in water pressure, which he can feel over his
entire body. Once when a fish swims past his shelter he
detects a brief turbulence its tail movements leave in the
wake, knowing at once that the source is biological. Other
sources, like slightly shifting currents, are hydrodynamic
and of abiotic origin. Although he has fallen overboard at
least a mile from any land, he knows instinctively when
the tide is changing, almost feeling the moon's gravita-
tional tug through changing forces in the surrounding
water. He can sense when the backwash from a distant

beach reaches him as a long exhalation.

These physical (actually, hydrodynamic) phenomena are being detected and monitored continuously, not only through specialized organs that also monitor temperature, but by thousands of setae — microscopic, hairlike mechanical sensory receptors on the surfaces of his body — each penetrating his shell and plugging into a neural connection inside. They keep track of such physical phenomena as direction and speed of water currents, the presence of eddies, and whether the origin of a patch of turbulence is abiotic or biological. Simultaneously, they interpret the signals received, alerting Sonny to physical fluxes in his surroundings and providing the necessary data to make decisions. In addition to these organs and their setae are two statocysts, one on each side near the front of the carapace at the base of the second antennae, and primarily involved in maintaining equilibrium. When Sonny fell overboard and was tumbling in the water column, he righted himself with their aid.

Tremulous, anamorphic flecks of dawn trickle down to him, prophesying the sun. The event is noted by other sea dwellers. There's a changing of shift: nocturnal creatures seek their lairs; others, chary of darkness and loving the light, emerge from their own hiding places. He decides to ignore his hunger and wait until dusk before leaving the shelter to forage. He's hungry but uneasy about venturing out in daylight, sensing intuitively that lobsters are crepuscular and nocturnal. Better wait until day's end, but how will he find food in dim light or its near-total absence? His eyesight has always been poor, especially in bright light, but he's about to discover a wonderful new chemical sensory system.

Lobsters have highly developed smell and taste,

these sensory systems being closely linked. The principal odor receptors are hairlike setae covering the antennules (the first antennae), the lobster's "nose." Chemoreceptor cells in these setae are adept at detecting amino acids in the water, the precursors of proteins, in addition to other compounds associated with food. Like hounds following scents, lobsters receive odors and move toward their source. Flicking the antennules pushes away previously smelled water and allows new water to flow past the chemoreceptive setae. Because there are two antennules, sensing the differential concentrations of a target odor allows a lobster to turn left or right toward the greater concentration.

Without Sonny's awareness these antennular chemoreceptors have been actively retrieving useful information. An enticing blend of odors has been drifting into the entrance of his shelter, many barely detectable and some clearly signaling food. They have arrived on the current then continued past, weakening with dilution. Most are unfamiliar. He waits anxiously for dusk.

Sonny discovers that he is also detecting odors through setae blanketing his mouthparts and legs, including the claws. Like those on the antennules these setae are packed with chemosensory receptors plugged into a specialized system of nerves. He's learning that his first two pairs of walking legs do more than walk; they serve as Swiss Army knives able to grasp and manipulate objects with tiny pincers and direct them to the mouthparts, and, of course, that setae on their surfaces contain touch and taste receptors. Humans can walk on their feet and receive tactile sensations through the soles, but their feet are worthless for tasting. Advantage to lobsters. He notices that while standing idly in the same place these miniature claws have been restlessly picking up items from the substrate, frantically testing them for food odors — separating, ripping, and snipping them — lifting tidbits to the three pairs of mouthparts to be tasted and masticated and if rejected then dropped, retrieved, manipulated again, and resubmitted, the mouthparts' taste receptors having final say. This behavior is autonomous, activated by odors emanating from organic compounds, amino acids in particular.

Sequestered in holes, fissures, and crevices on the substrate are Asian shore crabs, European green crabs, and Atlantic rock crabs. The place is a smorgasbord of crustacean delights. He has only to reach in, drag them out, crush them, and stuff himself. He then discovers he can excavate clams from the muddy and sandy bottoms and process them with his two major claws, each having a special function and design. He can crush the shells with the larger crusher claw, slice off chunks with the narrower cutter claw, and let the pincers of his first two pairs of walking legs take over to pick out the meat. The cutlery is in place. In short, a lobster comes equipped with all necessary tools for sensing, locating, capturing, preparing, and consuming food that seems to be everywhere. In the final stages of the sequence his mouthparts, esophagus, and gastric mill handle the levigating. These built-in advantages, combined with catholic tastes, make a lobster's gastronomic life easy.

7.

SONNY HAS QUICKLY ADAPTED to life as a lobster and enjoys having conquered gravity. He no longer limps and crawls to ambulate as he did on land, often collapsing from exhaustion after moving just a short distance or performing an easy task that ordinary humans would barely think about. It must be, he thought, similar to visiting the moon where the gravity is one-sixth that of Earth. What a pleasure!

One night while foraging he encounters another male lobster for the first time. This individual rushes at him with claws raised and shouting, "Put 'em up! Put 'em up!"

Startled, Sonny backs away, then examines his adversary from a distance. He can't see details in the darkness but recognizes the voice, despite having received the message telepathically. "Professor? Is it you?" he says. This is the first time he's tried speaking since the metamorphosis and is astounded that the process works. "We heard at the university that you'd drowned, that you fell off my uncle's lobster boat and never surfaced."

The other lobster has stopped a short distance away. He snorts, or tries to, a difficult feat underwater when lacking a conventional nose, lungs, and related paraphernalia. He says, "To paraphrase Twain, news of my demise has been greatly exaggerated. I stand here alive in claw and chitin. Who the hell are you? Tell me your name and station at once, or I promise I'll kick that telson so high into your tomalley you'll have to peel off your carapace to shit." He adds in a smaller voice: "I mean it, I really do."

"I'm Sonny, Professor. You probably don't remember, but I took your class in crustacean biology."

As if stimulating his memory the Professor touches a walking leg to the front of his carapace, the part that with permissible disregard of definitions might be called his head. "Ah yes. Sonny. We two were the sorriest freaks in the room. Me a hopeless cripple, you a. . .whatever. Still, I felt no special bond. In fact, in those days my Procrustean self sought to avoid others with disabilities, not offer succor. So, what do you want of me? I'm actually quite busy, not that anyone down here notices."

Sonny says, "I don't want anything. We just bumped into each other. It's a coincidence, that's all. I'll leave you alone," and he walks away in another direction, the Professor having confirmed that lobsters are innately anti-social, or that perhaps in the Professor's case his original human disposition has simply carried over unchanged.

Sonny has second thoughts and turns back. He asks the Professor to translate the sign posted at the dock underneath the aquarium that always holds a lobster during tourist season. It was he who instructed Uncle to nail it there, so he undoubtedly knows its meaning. The Professor stops rubbing his carapace. "Oh that. Yes, of course, *Und wenn du lange in einen Abrund blickst, blickt der Abgrund auch in dich hinein.* It's a quote of Nietzche's and says in English, 'And when you look long into the abyss, the abyss also looks into you.' Call it my inchoate premonition. At the time I'd been reading lots of philosophy along with reports in cellular biology on the regeneration of lost limbs, the science of which was, and still is, a mystery. I often wondered what it might be like to regrow a complex organ or appendage like my lost arm and leg as an amphibian or crustacean can do. We humans — and I fit that category at the time — consider ourselves 'higher' animals despite many of the so-called 'lower' forms seeming to be more advanced in some respects. Such arrogance!"

The Professor then slips into his lecturing voice. "The most interesting commentary I found was a story by Romeo Poole published in the December 1925 issue of *Weird Tales: The Unique Magazine* and republished in 1973 in the magazine *Fantasy Classics-4*. It's titled "A Hand from the Deep," and the narrative has a definite Frankensteinish feel. A quack named Dr. Whitby has amputated Simon Glaze's arm a little above the elbow following 'a smash-up over at the barrel-stave mill.' However, his objective is to have Glaze regrow the lost limb, not simply treat the healing stump. To that end Whitby injects him with 'glandular extracts' derived from lobsters and crayfish. During the extended treatment Whitby's institution is destroyed by an explosion and fire, and only Glaze survives. Subsequent caregivers are puzzled by his insistence that his stump be kept wet and that he be allowed cold baths several times daily. In a mere couple of weeks Glaze loses his speech and becomes brutish in manner and appearance, resembling a lobster in both respects. His behavior is lobsterly too. When stressed, for example, he retreats backward from his interlocuters. Glaze soon drowns in his bathtub. Although his brain had undergone metamorphosis and become crustacean, his breathing apparatus didn't keep pace. The good arm had turned into a lobster claw, and the stump had grown fingerlike projections showing evidence of eventually turning into a decapodish appendage. Definite progress in regenerative medicine, you could say, if only fictional, although still not encouraging."

The Professor pauses. "I notice you haven't said anything. Sorry for these digressions. Hope I haven't bored you. Okay, back to the present. So, Uncle is actually your uncle? Everyone at the dock called him Uncle too. On thinking back I see the family resemblance: you, him, and with a little imagination the sternman too."

"Homer is my cousin," Sonny says.

"Anyway," the Professor says, once again straying off the subject, "I never dreamed I'd someday become a lobster capable of regenerating appendages as a matter of course. When I stared too long at that lobster in the aquarium on the dock I began to believe it was staring back. When Uncle told me it was an illegal breeder and had to be released, I asked if I could go along for the ride, then fell overboard in a rogue swell the instant the lobster dropped from the sternman's hand, if it could be called his hand. Odd chap that sternman, a sort of Humpty-Dumpty with spindly arms and legs, very dexterous at his tasks."

Then abruptly back on track: "Obviously, you once were a big lobster with a color mutation. The one I stared at too intensely was considerably larger than average too, but conventionally pigmented. The sternman is your cousin, eh? That doesn't surprise me. Oh well. Here I am, and here you are, together in the same boat, in a manner of speaking. Evolution, that most confusing of palimpsests. Do you feel better about yourself after the metamorphosis, or worse?"

"Definitely better. I'm no longer handicapped. I could barely get around before."

"Same with me. As you remember, I labored through the halls of the university hobbling on a prosthetic leg, the empty sleeve of my sport jacket stuffed into the side pocket. Don't believe for a second I didn't hear the snickers of the students and see the disdain on the faces of the faculty, sometimes mixed with open disgust. Sadly, it wasn't always this way. I grew up on an Illinois farm, you see, and as a boy of twelve got caught in a corn picker my daddy was running. That particular one, which we'd rented for the harvest, was lacking an emergency stop, not unusual in some of the older models. Daddy had told me to jump off and check what might be causing the disturbing clanking sound we kept hearing from underneath the machine. He didn't shut it down because then we couldn't have identified the source. I was standing on the header prongs while it idled there in the field when Daddy went to light a cigarette and accidently activated the header. The combine lurched forward, sucked me in like a cornstalk, and chewed off an arm and a leg. For years afterward corn seemed so repulsive I couldn't even look at it, but the feeling eventually went away. Then, upon moving to New England I got so I could eat it now and again, at clambakes where it's served with a lobster and steamer clams."

Sonny says, "Weren't you married, Professor? I recall that you had a wife. After you disappeared she did too. At least, we never saw her on campus."

"Ha! My loyal wife!" The Professor gives a kind of snort and wipes his rostrum with his crusher claw. "Yes indeed. . .my wife. With the stealth of a spider, my wife waited a few weeks after my disappearance, eventually entrapping a man with a full set of appendages, or so I suspect. I wasn't around, you see. She probably divorced me *in absentia* and married him. Inevitable, I suppose. If true, I only hope the sonofabitch is suffering the way she made me suffer." He lifts his other claw, the cutter, to his face and scissors absently at his rostrum, probably the lobsterly equivalent of picking his nose.

"Think of it," says the Professor. "When I was still in human form, although presumably dead — or so my wife undoubtedly believed — I'm convinced that she absconded with a man who had four appendages. I presently have ten, but would she be impressed on seeing me now?" Sonny senses the Professor stretching out his claws sideways in the dark, first the left then the right. "On the one claw, doubtfully," he says. "On the other claw, a lobster with only four legs would be considered handicapped." He pauses and looks as thoughtful as is possible for a lobster. "At least I think so, but who can say? That lobster would be handicapped until its next molt and afterward merely deformed. Usually, more than one molt is necessary to regrow a regenerating appendage to normal size and full function."

8.

THE PROFESSOR SETTLES INTO his resting pose, abdomen curled under him, dorsal surface of his carapace leaning against a rock. The claws are crossed on his ventrum, walking legs spread out to the sides for balancing in the current. Over the months he and Sonny have encountered each other several times during nocturnal forays and become, if not exactly friends (a seeming impossibility for lobsters), at least tolerant acquaintances. Sonny has positioned himself nearby on the sandy bottom, standing lightly on his walking legs in the manner of a regular lobster. He has just asked the Professor a question and curiously awaits the reply.

"You ask what I think about? Important matters, my boy. I wonder if our European cousins represented by *Homarus gammarus* are outliving us on a Mediterranean diet. Also, does nose hair continue growing after death? What's my age in lobster years? Naturally, I'm curious if God resembles a crustacean. Why should we accept Michelangelo's depiction of Him as an old whitebearded Italian?

"I think about telepathic communication. Direct human-to-human speech underwater without an air interface is impossible. If the gas-filled spaces are

37

replaced by water they can no longer function as acoustic transformers converting sound pressure to particle displacement. All the required tissues and spaces used in air — lips, mouth, tongue, teeth, nasal and sinus cavities, lungs, vocal cords, larynx, pharynx, windpipe, soft palate, diaphragm, and a whole bunch of other stuff — are useless when flooded, and anyway they instantly disappear once you transition into a lobster. But communicate we formerlies do. . .somehow, telepathically. Can anything like sound be measured during one of our conversations? Are water molecules — the surrounding "particles" — induced to vibrate? These are open questions. The mode and mechanics of telepathic communication among us formerlies remains a mystery." He says this accompanied by what might have been a disdainful sniff, although sniffing is hard to detect, even for another lobster, when worked subtly through the antennules.

"Lately, however, I've been pondering our metamorphosis and reprising memories of stories and novels on the subject. Literary fiction offers many cases of transformations and translocations of various sorts. You and I and the other formerlies are exceptional among lobsters, of course, because we're living the switchover in real life." He raises a walking leg and scratches his rostrum. "At least I think so, presuming we and everything around us is real and not a dream. My favorite example is the nameless protagonist in Julio Cortázer's story "Axolotl" who becomes a habitual visitor to the obscure, humid little aquarium building at the Jardin des Plantes in Paris where he stares for hours at the axolotls on display. They become an obsession, and every day he parks his bicycle at the entrance, goes in, and watches them. He's fascinated by their human-like phalanges, their near-immobility, their vacant eyes that seem to stare back, and their fierce ennui. Suddenly, he finds himself on the other side of the glass, startled to have become an axolotl too. From this moment he knows he's destined to live among them, *to be* one of them.

"And in Nabokov's story 'La Veneziana' a young man enchanted by a sixteenth-century portrait of a girl who would have been about his own age is suddenly transferred into the painting, becoming a static image next to hers, trapped there forever. He tries looking to his left at the girl but is unable to swivel his head. He has become part of the scene, unfortunately depicted beside her in a 'ridiculous pose' that Nabokov declines to describe. Directly in front of our unlucky youth, and distinctly clearer than before, stretches the hall in which the painting hangs, the last and only view he will ever see.

"Perhaps most famous is Kafka's novella *The Metamorphosis* published in 1915, although in my opinion overrated. Cortázer's 'Axolotl' is much more compact, subtle, and sinuously creative. In Kafka's tale the protagonist, a young traveling salesman named Gregor Samsa, awakes in his family's apartment in Prague to find he's been transformed into a beetle of near-human dimensions. The event brings considerable shame to his parents and sister, who try half-heartedly to cope with this monstrosity as their new housemate. Only the charwoman is nonplussed. Gregor eventually dies of starvation allowing the family to celebrate, finally relieved of its burden.

"Oh yes, strange things happen, and not only in literature," says the Professor. "You and I are the proof. How did you come to be down here? Is your story similar to my own? No doubt you fell off Uncle's boat along with a lobster you'd been staring at in that aquarium on the dock, as I alluded in our first conversation. At least I presume so." He seems puzzled, although puzzlement is difficult to discern in lobsters.

"Almost identical." Sonny tells the Professor about his early life and involuntary exile to Suramoh Island, ending with a description of the transforming moment. "Every morning before leaving the dock with Uncle and Homer I stared at a big blond lobster in that aquarium beside the lobster pound, and I'd stare at it again after we came in and unloaded the catch. Couldn't take my eyes off it. Because it was breeding size, Uncle's legal duty was to release it at the end of the tourist season, same as in your case. The Department of Marine Resources allows the cooperative to keep one unusual lobster on display through the summer as a tourist draw. So, after the last of the tourists had left in early fall, Uncle transferred the lobster to his boat's livewell and he, Homer, and I embarked to sea to release it, the final trip before the boat went into winter drydock. I was holding the lobster preparing to let it go when I lost my balance and fell overboard. As I was sinking, having metamorphosed instantaneously into that lobster, Uncle stuck his head underwater and shouted some advice about quickly finding a hiding place. Well, here I am too. By the way, do you miss anything? I mean, from up there." Sonny points up with his cutter claw indicating the world above the surface.

"A few things, but I sure as hell don't miss being handicapped and shuffling through my days on a crutch trying to maintain balance with just one arm and one leg, hearing the sniggers and sensing the disrespect. It's like trying to fly on one wing. I'd much rather be a healthy, rambunctious lobster. Neither do I miss the gratis colonoscopy offered by the university that I declined upon turning forty-five. However, I do miss a cigar and snifter of rum after a nice dinner, and I miss cracking my knuckles, of course. Who doesn't?

"But hear, hear! No more depressing talk! On the bright side the lobster's gustatory horizon is limitless. We lobsters can digest nearly anything. The entire organic universe is grist for our gastric mills. Nothing makes us sick. We never get an ache in any of our three stomachs. There's no chance of contracting norovirus, ciguatera, or salmonella poisoning, and no such thing as 'bad' food. Everything on today's menus is rotten, you say? Bring it on! Practically speaking, it's impossible to be sickened by food or to starve."

"What about eating seaweed?" Sonny ventures. "I notice we don't do much of that."

"In moderation, my boy. The stuff's high in polyphenols. You can see what a *nori* diet did to the Japanese people, stunted their growth and turned their skin yellow. You might recall that I'm sort of a foodie," the Professor telepaths in a needlessly confidential tone. "Naturally, I continue to inventory the local dietary items and attempt to draw parallels with my former life when fine dining on a university professor's salary was nearly impossible. The choices down here aren't much better, but everything is sashimi and salty, which greatly simplifies choices. We lobsters mostly eat other invertebrates, which are isosmotic with seawater, same as ourselves, and therefore have a saltiness equal to seawater. The tunics of sea squirts — and hence the name of this group, the tunicates — are brimming with complex carbohydrates and taste a little like soggy soda crackers. Not bad, but in my opinion all sea squirt species are best consumed as appetizers.

"As for entrées we lobsters commonly enjoy, the

flesh of mussels and clams picked from their crushed shells has a rubbery consistency and turgor reminiscent of steak tartare. Small limpets and periwinkles swallowed whole are pretty much tasteless, although bigger ones are crunchy when consumed with their masticated shells. Same with welks. Welk flesh is rubbery like that of other mollusks, and the slime imparts an interesting aftertaste of garlic with a hint of butter and parsley. Seaweeds, of course, are high in iodine, and that comes through, as does umami, although the inevitable epibionts — those tiny animals and plants that attach to seaweeds and other organisms including us — render their flavor unpredictable. And, of course, flavor also varies with the species of algae, the botanical group to which seaweeds belong. Fishes all taste pretty much the same. They vary mainly in consistency: some are bonier or have tougher scales; others are exceptionally slimy or oily. We don't get much fresh fish. It's mostly scavenged carcasses.

"But my favorite meal is a newly molted rock crab. Nothing beats it. After that, young rock crabs captured while scavenging at night, often with some tasty morsel recently ingested, which adds an interesting condiment. Other crabs also are tasty. I like 'em all, yessir, I surely do. And after crabs, know what comes in second? Baby lobsters newly metamorphosed into the fourth growth stage, recently dropped out of the plankton and just learning to crawl along the bottom. The decapodal equivalent of toddlers, you could say."

He suddenly raises a claw. "Wait! Don't look at me like that! I see you about to protest, but hear me first. This discussion reminds me of an old theory. It states that the perfect food for a carnivorous animal is a healthy member of its own species. Why? Because all necessary nutrients and essential elements come prepackaged and consist entirely of what a conspecific — a member of one's own species — requires to nourish and build identical tissues. A ready-made balanced diet, you might say. Now, not all scientists subscribe to this thinking, but if it holds any truth then the healthiest food for a lobster is another lobster.

"I'll remind you what Stebbing wrote in his 1893 paper on the natural history of the Crustacea. I taught his work in the classroom, remember? Noting that young lobsters (and old ones too) are sometimes cannibalistic, he stated: 'We cannot afford to find fault with their juvenile morals, since similar practices have been followed, in some stages of society, by human beings themselves.' So, my lad, abjure yourself of silly taboos and accept that to a lobster other lobsters are nutritious *and* delicious!" After a moment he adds, "I must be getting senile. I'm able to remember quotes like that and events from the distant past, but recent memories last only several days. In this sense I've become very lobsterly. Of course, I've always suffered from prosopagnosia, so no surprise I can't recall people's faces, or those of lobsters either. Don't take it personally. Strange. . . ." His voice trailed off.

"Anyway," he says, seeming to return from a distant place, "stage-four baby lobsters, little lobsters that look just like adults, are the perfect dessert, every bit as satisfying as juvenile rock crabs. Remember those Swiss chocolates that have a crunchy shell and a soft, squishy center? They're similar. And now, seeing as how you're my guest I hasten to offer tasty morsels from the sea's bounty." He leans forward holding out something macerated and gooey. "Another sea squirt? These are newly gathered and very healthy. Remember what I just said: lots of carbs in their tunics." He shoves one clumsily in Sonny's face.

9.

SONNY HAS BEEN A resident of the Gulf for quite a while. At least it seems so. How long, exactly? Who knows or cares? Lobsters don't track such matters. However, his only friends remain the Professor and another formerly who goes by Day Tripper. This assumes their rare inter-actions actually constitute friendships and not merely passing acknowledgment. The Professor and Day Trip-per dislike each other, ruling out regular get-togethers. The Professor thinks of Day Tripper as an uneducated boor; Day Tripper considers the Professor a snob and a weakling bereft of streetwise experience and pathetically ignorant of the female sex. Sonny remains neutral, not wishing to upset either.

He and the Professor are foraging in a patch of mus-sels, conversing while cracking shells. Sonny idly asks the Professor if he ever feels lonely and wishes he had more friends.

"Don't be ridiculous," says the Professor. "I refused to have friends as a human and still do. I've never met another human or lobster worth knowing. In my for-mer life I reveled in *schadenfreude*, telling people that humanity could kiss my rosy-red ass, but for obvious reasons anything associated with red is taboo among lobsters, at least to formerlies. Despite our colorblindness the conflation of red with being boiled alive conjures unpleasant feelings."

"Thanks for the comment on friendship," says Sonny sarcastically. "I always knew you cared."

The Professor, who is has just taken a break and leaned back, his carapace against a rock, raises his claws in a haughty "excuse me" gesture. He's agitated, breathing rapidly through his twenty pairs of gills. "Well, shit, don't take it personally," he says, as he rolls onto his dactyls and returns to cracking mussels with exaggerated verve. "That's how it is. I can't change anything, and too bad if your precious feelings are hurt. Anyway, I was just mulling over how refreshing it is to live where politics don't exist and strife is strictly personal. There aren't any lobster armies attacking rival armies, no lobster nations with their hegemony. We're back to hunter-gatherer times. Even your pal Day Tripper seems satisfied to take events as they come without any plotting and scheming."

Sonny says, "He and I aren't actual pals, just acquaintances, like the two of us. He was probably always like that except with his homeboys. Not everyone dreams of conquering the world."

"I take it you didn't know him before."

"No, and when we meet he always recounts the story of how he became a lobster. He remembers all the details but not that I've heard them before. It doesn't matter because afterward I don't remember them anyway."

The Professor says, "Maybe this is evidence of becoming senile before our time, except this *is* our time. Borges taught us that words are symbols assuming a shared memory. It's why nothing relevant of life remains after memory departs. Well, my gastric mill hasn't stopped grinding, so I still must be hungry. Resume the feast, eh?" As he says this he cracks another mussel.

Sonny asks the Professor why he so dislikes Day Tripper, seeing that the two have met only a few times and are pretty much absent from each other's lives.

"I can't stand being around him. One reason is his crudeness," says the Professor. "He seems able to introduce 'fuck' or 'fucking' into every sentence. To what purpose? Last I saw of him he was whining about his wife and now putative widow 'fucking' the neighbor while he was at work, cuckolding him as he slaved away earning their daily bread. The neighbor, he'd said, was on disability and home all day. I don't believe the wife was working either. Attribute the blame-shame game to propinquity while shouldering none himself, eh? A sordid story very different from my own in which the wife was indeed evil and completely at fault despite my not knowing exactly how her situation turned out. Not that I'm biased and unwilling to give her benefit of the doubt."

Sonny ignores this last comment and says, "Too bad Day Tripper can't demand conjugal rights and visit her himself. She could get an aquarium and keep him around. But a woman and a lobster?" He expels a lobsterly snort and crunches another mussel.

"Such liaisons aren't impossible, in fiction at least." Sonny recognizes when the Professor is about to muse on some arcane subject and venture into the intellectual weeds, usually leaving him to struggle along behind.

Sure enough, the Professor says, "Have you read Guillaume Lecasble's work? No? Lecasble is a French polymath: writer, filmmaker, and painter. His novella titled *Lobster* opens with a scene of male passengers aboard the *Titanic* trailing after the lovely but tragic

Angelina. They follow her from deck to deck like neighborhood mongrels sniffing a delicate poodle in heat, all but howling, slavering, and pissing out their hormonal grief against the chair legs. But Angelina has eyes for none, having slipped into a deep depression. Despite many past lovers she has never achieved orgasm. Meanwhile, Lobster, the other protagonist, is short-timing it in the ship's galley. He and his parents, caught in traps, have been taken aboard as future cuisine for the first-class passengers.

"Lobster's mom and dad have recently made their appearance at the dinner hour and are reduced to empty shells, and Lobster himself is partway into the pot when *Titanic* strikes that iceberg and tilts. The pot tumbles off the stove, and a half-cooked but still living Lobster, tinted a rosy pink but thankfully not bright red, is dumped onto the galley floor. In the ensuing flood he clutches one of Angelina's legs as she climbs a stairway from the dining room to an upper deck. Lobster recognizes her as the passenger who has just eaten Dad and is thinking vengeance. However, she exudes a strange sexual attraction despite being human.

"He scrabbles higher underneath Angelina's dress and pulls down her panties. He flutters his antennae — presumably the second, 'feeler' antennae — in her crotch, making her labia resonate. As an aside, we can only imagine what his antennules are sniffing. Using one of his claws — Lecasble doesn't reveal which, but no doubt the cutter claw — he snips away the satiny fabric seeing 'the two separate pieces floating soft as seaweed in the swirl.'

"Then the humping commences, crustacean swimmerets to mammalian pudendum. There's no mention of gonophoric penetration, but the coupling successfully reaches a rhythmic dénouement. Meanwhile, Lobster is gripping Angelina's pubic hairs in one claw, I'm guessing the crusher, and manipulating her clitoris with the other, likely the more maneuverable cutter, as they bob vertically between air and water, allowing each to alternately breathe. Angelina attains orgasm, after which she gives Lobster a sort of blowjob by putting his head in her mouth and running her tongue around his eyes and mouthparts. Those digital manipulations of Lobster's, along with his rubescent carapace and lingering cologne of steaming bay leaf from the boiling pot, had really turned her on. They're in love.

"Naturally, she sneaks Lobster aboard the lifeboat while he's still underneath her dress, but he inadvertently falls into the sea. The two lovers are separated, never to meet again. Lobster does get vengeance, though: once submerged he discovers the corpse of the woman who has recently eaten Mom and in turn eats her.

"Lobster and Angelina search the world in vain for one another. Angelina, consumed by grief, eventually drowns herself in the Seine; Lobster's end arrives with celerity when he tumbles into a pot of soup cooking on a stove and is eaten by his human friend who has been helping locate Angelina and is secretly in love with her. Why waste a lobster dinner, right? Keep in mind that the author of *Lobster* is a Frenchman. Lobsters aren't the only nation of creatures who divide Earth's resources into food and sex before finding them indistinguishable."

"That's quite a story. Too bad I won't get to read it," says Sonny.

"Indeed," the Professor telepathizes loudly. "And while I recounted Lecasble's tale for your edification and enjoyment you surreptitiously hogged more than your fair share of mussels. Another reason friendship is over-rated." He spins around and gives Sonny an aggressive blast of urine in the face.

Sonny jumps in surprise. On noting the remark he had considered it one of the Professor's bleak stabs at humor, but now realizes that his dining companion is truly pissed off. The professor then does something remarkable. He assumes a submissive position, lying on his ventrum with all ten legs outstretched and claws touching. "I'm sorry," he says. "You're right. I was once a very lonely man, although as a lobster I feel much more confident being by myself. We lobsters actually prefer it. Having a friend, though, is nice. I must get accustomed to the idea." He scrambles back onto his walking legs. "Claw bump?" he says.

"Claw bump," says Sonny.

10.

THE PROFESSOR LEANS BACK and becomes silent, seemingly focused on plucking off small, exiguous objects attached to his ventrum using the pinchers of his first two pairs of walking legs. They scissor earnestly, robotically. Finally, he says to Sonny, "On first thought, you might seek to better impress by introducing an occasional foreign word into your dialogues, preferably French. On second thought, forget such ridiculosities. Nobody down here would care. On third thought, up there either. Anyhow, you probably don't know any foreign words.

"Admittedly, I pine for certain aspects of intellectual life, not the social part, mind you, but interaction with others from a distance and under tightly circumscribed conditions. To this end I've been thinking of starting a newsletter directed at the Gulf's residents. The aim is to provide information of interest to both long-time citizens and recently arrived immigrants. All these unfortunates have left behind key elements of their lives as humans. Picture a ballerina without toe shoes and tutu, a vampire *sans* incisors and cape. We are seriously disadvantaged down here in terms of amenities. Naturally, I feel their distress. Perhaps a column devoted just to females: who among us is berried and the projected release date of her larvae, who is suffering postpartum depression, that sort of thing, probably a common condition in a species that breeds with such exuberant pullulation. Maybe even an advice column. And dining recommendations, of course. What's your opinion?"

Sonny says, "I don't think anyone will care. As lobsters go, not even formerlies are reliable readers."

The Professor gazes up, twisting his eyestalks. Sonny recognizes the sign: he's drifting toward one of his tortuous riffs. "The underlying problem is that nobody reads anymore, especially fiction. It's tragic, really. Reading fiction is such a rewarding pastime. Each author of fiction releases into the intellectual atmosphere a product of unique flavor, odor, and temperature. It's then the task of the reader to pick over this smorgasbord and through ingesting the poems and tales enjoin them organically. To me, for example, T. S. Eliot's poems have a standoffish, prissy taste, their temperature a little frigid for this palate. I prefer warmer fare. The poems of Dylan Thomas, in contrast, deliver sparks from a master wordsmith's anvil. Read carefully because one of them might put out an eye. Patrick Chamoiseau's prose is a hallucinogenic banquet presented in semi-civilized surroundings, unexpected and slightly dangerous to the palette. Particularly delicious are his yummy creole women, who without warning appear before us hot, Black, and bitter. Ah, and I can't omit the stories of Barry Hannah, best imbibed in a Southern get-your-shirt-tore bar while sipping a glass of sour-mash whiskey and packing a sidearm. Maylis de Kerangal's protagonists dress and behave like other women, but their minds give off tastes and scents that are anything but ordinary. And if you enjoy perfervid introspection combined with a smoky sourness, spend time inside the stories of

Clarice Lispector. I could go on. The highway traveled by literature has no beginning, no end, and infinite offramps. Take any at random and be delighted."

The Professor stands as if about to deliver a lecture. "Okay, so lobsters aren't big readers. I accept that. But if they're incapable of conceiving time — that is, the past and future — then shouldn't we at least encourage them to experience the present in all its manifestations? This is a newsletter's or newspaper's *raison d'être*. It's the vacuum I was hoping to fill."

Sonny says, "I guess so, but let's be practical. How will you write, print, and distribute this newsletter or newspaper? And how will you go about gathering news? Recruit a bunch of younger formerlies and designate them cub reporters? That's not a joke. I'm serious."

"Yes, of course you are." As a human the Professor had a mannerism of pulling on an earlobe when perplexed. These days he touches the dactyl of a walking leg to an eyestalk. "Big problems, all." He examines his claws. "With these clumsy appendages, cursive is out of the question. We could use local ink, I suppose. Many creatures around here — the octopuses and squids, for example — manufacture it, but how to solve the dilution issue? And I can't see a squid giving up its ink voluntarily. You know what that means." He makes a slashing motion with a walking leg across his nonexistent throat. "Anyway, what would we use for paper? Too bad there's no Internet down here, then we could have subscribers email us their stories."

"Then you wouldn't need a newsletter, just a chatroom."

"I suppose you're right. It's depressing, not being able to deploy the skills acquired during a lifetime's training and experience. Oh well." He throws up his claws in frustration. "Nonetheless, it's fun to dream. I spent hours pondering a name for my publication and was finally inspired by recalling one of Italo Calvino's novels. The Baron of Rondò, protagonist of *The Baron in the Trees*, is believed by most to be mad because as a child he relinquished life on the ground to live in trees, growing to adulthood among the branches and never descending. However, from his leafy heights he offered to the surrounding community useful advice and a calming philosophy and came to be loved and respected. He communicated his thoughts, in part, through a weekly newspaper titled *The Bipeds' Monitor*, later changed to *The Reasonable Vertebrate*. I had intended to call my circular *The Reasonable Invertebrate* in the Baron's honor, which seems both timely and appropriate and because, well, I sort of identify with him, another outsider: I'm a lobster living at the bottom of the ocean, he's a baron who lived in trees instead of in the mansion on his estate. Then there's the word 'reasonable.' Who couldn't admire the absurdity? Lord knows, little of what happens around here could be termed reasonable by anyone's definition, wouldn't you agree?"

Without waiting for Sonny's reply, the Professor continues, "I suppose the most unsettling issue is whether an invertebrate protagonist can be an unreliable narrator in its own tale. Glimmers of consciousness have been imputed in nonhuman vertebrates capable of deception, so what it comes down to is this: to be an unreliable narrator requires the capacity to lie, raising the question, are invertebrates inveterate truth-tellers? If so, how dull. Of course, beings such as ourselves — formerlies, I mean — dragging remnant baggage of humanity, are incapable of assessing the matter in an unbiased way. Only true lobsters could do this, the resident beings you colorfully call 'homies,' and we have no evidence of their capacity to reason at even an elementary level, much less imagine and plot future situations with devious intent." He crudely scratches his telson with the pointed dactyl of a fifth walking leg. "Another example of the dilemma with which the philosopher Thomas Nagel burdened us when pondering what it's like to be a bat. His conclusion? Only a bat can ever know.

"On reconsidering Nagel's essay, I realize that I don't even know what being a lobster is like, except tangentially. I react to stimuli as a lobster does. I eat what lobsters eat, travel as they do, breathe water and expel it through gills. . .but I still think like a human. I'll say this, however: living as a lobster is a helluva lot easier. For instance, changing apartments in the old days was a nightmare. There I was, a cripple, trying to pack stuff one-handed, then lifting it one-handed and carrying the box up or down stairs one-handed on one leg. Of course, I had no friends to assist, and hiring a moving company on a professor's salary was usually prohibitive. I'd pay a couple of students instead, and surreptitiously they would break my things. These days? No furniture, no books and papers, no victuals including my former wine collection, no memorabilia, no bags to pack. . . .Move out and move in somewhere else. I try to find a vacant shelter to avoid conflict, but if it becomes necessary I can evict a smaller occupant using appropriate threats gleaned by observing such conflicts."

Sonny says, "But as humans we didn't share common traits with lobsters."

"My dear boy, of course we did! Consider the obvious synapomorphies. Our segmented construction for instance, not to mention our paired appendages. You must admit that humans and lobsters are built on a similar plan."

Sonny says dubiously, "Well, we still have to worry about the dangers."

"What dangers? You only need to avoid lobster traps. And, of course, left behind are any concerns about crossing busy streets, dying in airplane crashes and terrorist attacks, tumbling down stairs, being stuck in broken elevators, choking on a bite of steak. . . .In fact, all told it's pretty safe around here."

"According to Uncle, lobsters must beware of big cods swooping down and swallowing us."

"Crabshit," says the professor. "Don't believe any of it. The Gulf of Maine has turned into a bottom-up ecosystem. The cod and other top predators have been fished nearly to ecological irrelevance. Sure, at one time there were big cods that ate lobsters, sucked us right out of our shelters, and woe to any crustacean stupid enough to be strolling the seafloor unaware. However, we've moved up in the sea's zoological hierarchy since the groundfishery collapsed. We've joined the middle class and have our very own strand in the web of life. Put simply, we're everywhere, the Gulf of Maine's equivalent of the cockroach.

"Anyway, back to my idea of a newsletter. I thought I might include travel news gained by interviewing Gulf residents who have gone to interesting places and returned with stories and descriptions of the events they experienced during their peregrinations. Everyone appreciates a good adventure tale. Those have been popular since earlier times when dragons and other monsters lurked everywhere, including enormous lobsters.

Imagine the fear in every sailor's heart. I might even recount some of these legends and tales.

"For example, there's Conrad Gessner's *Icones Animalium Aquatilium in mari & dulcibus* published in 1560. In English that's *Illustrations of Aquatic Animals of Marine and Freshwaters*. *Icones* comes from the Greek and means likenesses, which today we might translate as images or illustrations. Gessner included a quasi-accurate illustration of a lobster, although of gigantic size. He referred to it as *Astaci Marini* and said the Germans called it *Humer*. The term 'lobster' in modern German is *Hummer*. This particular form of outsize lobster had been described a couple of decades earlier by a Swede, Olaus Magnus. The section titled 'Among the Orkney and Hebrides islands' of his *A Marine Chart and Description of the Northern Countries and the Wonders They Contain, Meticulously Made in the Year 1539* has a brief comment in Latin. The accompanying drawing depicts a specimen slightly larger than a human lying atop a bearded man, apparently in the act of devouring him. Gessner quotes Magnus as saying of the beast that 'it is huge and so strong that it would suffocate — he meant, drown — a swimming man captured by a claw.' A detail in section D of his map depicts a gigantic lobster holding in one raised claw a fully-dressed man. Truly scary, eh? As an interesting aside, Magnus took issue with his illustrator, complaining that all the walking legs had pincers, which of course is true only of the first two pairs, not the third and fourth pairs, and that the 'tail' (abdominal section) has too many segments. He was quite the observer! Nonetheless, Gessner republished the image without comment or changes.

"Going back in history still further, even the heroes

of ancient days were impressionable. You might remember from my crustacean biology class a little tale I wrote featuring Alexander the Great. I based it on one of the many legends that sprang up about Alexander in the years after he died. My idea originated from the several iterations of the Armenian *Alexander Romance*. I had written it in a fanciful literary style, purely fictional, of course, although no less so than the *Alexander Romance* itself. As you probably recall, I made copies and passed them out to the class, wrongly assuming my students would find the effort amusing. Quite the contrary in that era of political correctness."

"I remember your story," says Sonny. "I thought it was funny. I also remember a later incident when animal-rights activists on campus, angry that you depicted Alexander's horse as a sex object, protested and boycotted your year-end lecture in the auditorium accompanied by the dissection of a lobster."

"Quite right. Getting back to my foray into literature. Without the manuscript in front of me, I'll have to wing it. Anyway, my little riff was based on one adventure in particular in which Alexander encounters giant lobsters, the last animals and monstrosities he sees during his trip to the edge of the world. They're as big as the boats transporting his army across a lake, and fifty-four men are lost when one of these creatures surfaces and pulls them under.

"That was an adventure Alexander probably should have never undertaken. His three wisemen-advisers beg him not to go, telling him the risk is too great. Who knows what dangers might be encountered in lands never before seen by humans? And upon reaching the edge of the world, what then? Is it a precipice overlooking infinity?

"Alexander tells them they're worrywarts and pussies.

He says he'll be fine and that his plans are firm. He intends to leave nearly everyone and everything behind, taking just a small army of his bravest and truest soldiers led by reasoned, experienced generals. Alarmed, one adviser says, 'But Majesty, what about your harem? Will you be leaving your fourscore and eight fair ladies here?'

"'Of course, silly man!' says Alexander in his southern Macedonian drawl. 'I'll substitute a few husky stableboys who aren't afraid of roughing it.'

"The second adviser pipes up. 'And the generals, Majesty, what might they think of this?'

"Alexander finds the question puzzling. 'You mean, will they be envious? If so, they may bring their own stableboys or acquire them along the way. You know us Macedonians, we're quite open-minded when out conquering. Spoils of war and all that.'

"The third adviser speaks. 'But Majesty, isn't there someone you love and whom you'll miss and pine for?'

"Alexander answers as follows. 'I love only my horse Bucephalus, but he'll be going with me. In case you're wondering, our relationship will be platonic. There's no horsing around while on a mission. At such times we follow strict protocol: I mount him only from the side, an angle that makes penetration impossible, and in this way we set an example for the troops about what it means to separate rider from horse.'"

11.

TIME HAS PASSED SINCE Sonny and the Professor last met, not unusual for solitary animals such as American lobsters. It could have been months or years. Time doesn't mean much to decapods, evidently including those of the tentative subspecies *Homarus americanus olim*, commonly called "formerlies." Several seasons — way more than a few — have come and gone, that much is certain, but lobsters aren't big on archiving history. At last these two have come together in seven fathoms at a large rock blanketed with sea squirts. Following the usual preliminaries during which the Professor half-heartedly challenges him to fight and Sonny again introduces himself, Sonny has asked the Professor how he manages to keep track of his observations. "I don't," the professor says, shoving a sea squirt into his mouthparts. "If I haven't already told you, a lobster's memory, at least of agonistic encounters, only lasts a week. For everything else, who knows?"

"I forgot you told me," Sonny says.

"Well, there you go. I do a lot of backfilling. That's backing and filling, a lot of stopping and starting, starting and stopping, and then I usually forget anyway. Being underwater isn't helpful. Living at fathom depth I can't fathom which might be worse, ink running perpetually or no Internet service. How can anyone living down here possibly retain status as a *marquer de paroles*? By the way, what's your name?"

"Sonny. And what's it mean, that term you just mentioned in French?"

"Right. . . .Sonny. That term is the self-description of Patrick Chamoiseau, a *Martiniquais* who writes very original novels. 'Mark with words' is the literal translation. Chamoiseau translates it as 'word-scratcher,' which he prefers to 'writer' when describing his profession. However, what it all means after distillation to just the essentials is that trying to be a word-scratcher in these parts is a real bitch. Incidentally, have you recently noticed a deviant buzz in my delivery?"

"Nossir, just the usual lisp."

"God*dammit*, and I've worked so hard to acquire, you know, the international language of lobsters. I wonder if others — other lobsters, I mean — notice. Never mind. Who cares? They aren't exactly mental giants." He lifts a second walking leg and tugs at an eyestalk with the pinchers.

Sonny says he's curious about his heritage, and considering his strange earlier life he'd like to talk about Mutha and see if the Professor has any insight into his background, possible something that he, Sonny, has not yet considered. The matter has become bothersome, making him despondent. He tells the professor what's on his mind and that he's depressed.

The Professor settles into his usual resting position with his back against a rock, abdomen curled underneath, claws crossed over his ventrum. He says, "I have nothing to offer you, dear boy, except other flavors of melancholy.

They vary only in degrees of bitterness. Nonetheless, let's have a try, shall we? Your mom, I take it, is a 'comebacker,' not an ordinary revenant who has merely crawled out of the grave before feeling the force of that first shovelful of earth." He makes a clumsy aquatic equivalent of air-quotes using opposing walking legs.

He continues in his lecturing voice. "A 'comebacker' is a rare specimen whose transition has occurred in reverse, from lobster to a quasi-human characterized by hybrid lobster-human traits that some scientists think might have epigenetic origins. Among these are the eyes, which are beady, black, and buggy.

"Other crustacean-like features include the sharp, bumpy, narrow rostrum, practically a spiny nose, except it doesn't function as one. So far as I can tell from studying my own, it doesn't function as anything in particular. It's simply there. Then consider the sedentary life-style. Let's tick off some other characteristics, such as lobster-claw hands and often feet too (ectrodactyly). Add in a surficial condition in which the unusually thick and plastic epidermis (by human standards) is shed and renewed periodically. This is extreme scleroderma and analogous to molting. Don't leave out chronic imbal-ance (disequilibrium), limbs that are rachitic and also weak (quadriparesis) on land, and stiff neck syndrome (torticollis). In addition, comebackers suffer extreme nearsightedness and farsightedness (anisometropia) and are colorblind (achromatopsia). They prefer frequent immersion in chilly water to living in air for extended periods, although water that's not excessively cold. To most, sixty-two degrees Fahrenheit as ideal. Like both humans and lobsters they thermoregulate, moving away from undesirable temperatures. When seeking living quarters the predilection is for tight spaces (claustro-philia). In common with ordinary lobsters, comebackers shun light and are pretty much crepuscular and noc-turnal. In terms of personality they're self-centered, chauvinistic, antisocial, quarrelsome and combative, chronically depressed, and display an overall tendency to drag their asses around blaming the world for their unsatisfactory predicament.

"As I've said before, a lobster considers the ocean floor to be a smorgasbord where everything alive or dead is edible. A comebacker feels the same. Any of this sound like Mom? The histories of comebackers are always linked to humans who drown at sea: victims of ship sinkings and plane crashes, drunks who topple over the railings of cruise liners. . .that sort. Drowning being a minor cause of death in human societies, it's one rea-son comebackers are rare and might explain why their neighbors think of them simply as deformed, eccentric humans. Proposed scenario: a drowning victim newly become a corpse sinks to the bottom of the Gulf of Maine later to be discovered by a wandering lobster who stares too long into its eyes and finds itself on land mas-querading as a human. These beings appear to ordinary people as monstrosities to be avoided, feared, ridiculed, and suspected of participating in odd or even satanic rit-uals. Could this have been your mother's story? I add that in the old Nordic sagas and songs, to drown was 'to be at the bottom with the lobster.'"

"Mutha never said. I only know she's real old and once had a job in a cannery picking lobster meat out of the cooked shells. She told me she used the pincers of her first two pairs of walking legs. With four appendages going at once I bet Mutha was a helluva lobster picker.

And because the light hurts our eyes, she and I were often active at night. Some suspected us of collecting roadkill and taking it home to eat."

"No doubt," the professor says thoughtfully. "No doubt. Language is such a precarious tool for communication, and when words and phrases are captious or flipped upside-down, interpretation is especially difficult. Goethe, on his deathbed, cried, *Mehr Licht!* Did he mean that his own light was fading, or was he demanding that the curtains of the room be opened? Who knows? What could it mean to say that a lobster is 'invited to table' when the options are to share a meal or be the meal? And consider this irony: the instrument used by humans to break a crusher claw the better to pick the meat is called a 'claw crusher.'"

Sonny directs the Professor back to the subject of his question. "But how did she get here? Mutha, I mean."

"What's that? Right, okay. It's puzzling, and I'm not entirely sure. Allow me to restate my hypothesis in different terms. Think of staring into the abyss except in reverse. The reverse abyss effect is manifested when an ordinary lobster comes across the corpse of a drowned person and stares too long into its open eyes. Then that lobster might suddenly find itself on land making a half-telsoned try at living as a human. Does it make sense now?"

"No. I'm still confused."

"Right. Well, me too," says the Professor. He begins nervously grooming his antennules, lowering them repeatedly and dragging them one at a time through the pads of his mouthparts. He's doing this to detach microbiotic slime and keep the chemosensory receptor cells of the setae clean and unobstructed. Is he conscious of his actions? Probably not. Think of a man who having just finished dinner absently wipes his moustache to remove any taste and olfactory residue of prime rib and truffle mashed potatoes before kissing his date and risk offending the chemosensory receptors in her nose and mouth.

The Professor is clearly distressed about not being able to sort through the details of Sonny's lineage. He starts babbling, taking a stab at being simultaneously poetic and philosophical. "This is the sea. It has no remembrance, no pity or remorse, no sense of time or place because it's complete within its cold wetness, unforgiving and uncaring. It swallows and dissolves all that tumbles into it then smacks its lips wanting more. Its needs are insatiate, and in the end it will drown and devour everything, including the land." He stands tall on his walking legs and points his crusher claw dramatically at Sonny. "And you and I are doomed to live here. The air? Its lightness and near-absence of density? Gone. You'll never taste it again." He turns abruptly away, striding daintily forth on the tips of his dactyls, abstruse moonlight glinting off his patination. The dénouement is unmistakable; too bad there's no cape to swing across his shoulders, or shoulders to receive it.

12.

THE PROFESSOR HAS GIVEN Sonny a blow-by-blow description of a lobster fight's choreography, its regimented foreplay of dance steps, feints and touches, and the chemical signals deployed in dominance and fear. Ever the academic, he once during this disquisition veers into the agonistic patterns of other species, remarking casually that ghost crabs facing off on a beach and trying to intimidate each other produce rumbling sounds from their gastric mills; in human terms, by purposely making their tummies growl. With obvious satisfaction, the Professor had quipped: "You could call these agonistic displays 'bluster by borborygmus.'"

It was inevitable, that first fight, but when it came Sonny was fully prepared. Along with how the fight was destined to proceed, the Professor had explained the possible results, for example, knowing when to put up your dukes and when to beat dactyls, also known as folding your hand, turning telson, and getting the hell outta Dodge. Neither dominance hierarchies nor territories exist in free-living lobster societies, so there's no real status to be gained from winning fights. However, it's relevant to remain true to your more obstreperous hormones, so go for it.

And besides, being a dominant male is advantageous, principally by having your choice of shelter spaces, even evicting a resident lobster to gain it, and by catching the eyes of lady lobsters anxious to molt and then mate. Females prefer winners over losers and can distinguish a dominant male by the odor of his urine. In evolutionary terms, being dominant helps assure the propagation of your lineage by out-reproducing rivals. Sonny supposes he ought to consider his legacy in this light, although it somehow doesn't seem important. Who cared? So far as he knew, only the Professor, who has paradoxically declined to participate in evolution's rat race. Having lost appendages as a human, he was loathe to experience the same as a crustacean despite the capacity to regenerate them. Not worth it, he's told Sonny. "I intend to molt a few more times, maybe get up to fifteen pounds. Bigger lobsters are less vulnerable to predation and usually can choose shelter spaces without a fight. Then I'll retire to the abyss where nothing happens of any consequence and you rarely encounter a conspecific, especially of your own size. Lobsters that big are rare everywhere, and those of any size are rare in the abyss. A reclusive life would suit me fine." However, he went on, Sonny, being still a young lobster, needs to prosper and broadcast his seed. Therefore, prior to engaging in clawcuffs he should assess his prospective opponent in a calculated, rational way. It wasn't very difficult for a reasoning invertebrate like him. Actual battle tactics would come automatically from a blend of instinct and experience.

There were four items on the assessment check-list. First, compare your opponent's size with your own. According to the Professor, data show that a five per-cent difference gives the larger combatant a ninety-five percent chance of winning. Retreat if the other guy is even a teensie bit bigger. Second, take note of your opponent's claws. Increasing disparity in crusher claw size has a negative effective on the duration of fights: the bigger the relative claw of one opponent, the shorter the contest. Here again, size matters. Retreat if the other challenger's crusher claw is bigger than yours. Third, if you decide to fight, try estimating whether you're likely to win quickly, thereby avoiding the exhaustion and possible injury of a prolonged tussle. Fights generally last up to thirty minutes in contests between closely matched combatants. However, a contest can sometimes last twice that, interrupted by short breaks.

Fourth, is the challenger familiar? Have you fought him before? If so and you lost, you'll remember him by the scent of his urine and instinctively retreat, point being that you're likely to lose again. These memories of opponents last only about a week, so pay close attention to the first three assessments before risking getting your telson kicked. Although lobsters can recognize other lobsters as individuals, winners of agonistic encounters don't seem to remember past opponents. Sure, you can regenerate a lost leg, but it still takes time and a couple of molts before the new appendage attains normal size and function. The process might take two or more years. Additionally, your shell could be punctured in combat and you risk "bleeding" to death from leaking hemolymph, the arthropodal analogue of blood. There were other factors to consider, so obvious they needed only superficial discussion: your molt state, physical condition, and prior experience.

The Professor told Sonny to welcome every opportunity to molt and grow. This means moving into warmer water in late spring. The higher temperature promotes growth. And eat well. Challenges to fight diminish with body size, and the bigger you become the fewer the lobsters you'll encounter who present serious threats. Most will take your dominance for granted and grace-fully depart the field of battle, maybe after a half-hearted antennal lashing or hesitant meral spread. The Profes-sor explains that this latter gesture is an agonistic threat display in which opposing lobsters open and raise the claws and spread them wide, supposedly flashing the pale underside of the merus (another leg segment) for emphasis. He adds that this flashing aspect has not been confirmed experimentally, only surmised, and seems dubious considering the lobster's poor vision, dimness of the undersea environment, and the fact that lobsters are mostly active at night. A meral spread in darkness would appear to be useless if deployed as a visual signal.

Finally, he mentioned again that adult lobsters can remember the outcome of an agonistic encounter up to a week. If you meet a former combatant after that length of time and he seems to have forgotten and wants to start again, well, he has and the two of you will. Memories of agonistic encounters by juveniles last only four days before they're again ready to scuffle. Oh, the fleeting bravado of youth!

Thus prepared, when the moment arrives Sonny is ready. One night as he's loafing in his shelter a potential rival emerges from darkness into glancing caustics of moonlight on the sand patch at his entrance. This other lobster is almost his clone in terms of body and crusher claw size. He seems energetic, healthy, alert. His shell is clean with only a few epibionts stuck to his carapace. He buzzes but doesn't speak. A homeboy, Sonny thinks, not a formerly. This means no negotiation possible. Instinct alone is on the table, it's to be nature, mandible and claw. Flee and lose his shelter or fight and be evicted anyway if he loses.

He steps confidently out his entrance and into the arena where he and his opponent warily circle one another, bouncing like boxers on the dactyls of their walking legs. They stop, now face to face, immobile as statues and standing tall on the tips of their walking legs, each trying to gain a height advantage to appear bigger and dominant. Fights follow a stereotyped sequence, and here is the first opportunity for one or the other to retreat; neither does. They slowly touch claws, tentatively box. Another inflexion point to retreat or escalate; the moment passes. They piss in each other's faces, antennules flicking rapidly, each sniffing in the other's scent. Their gills and swimmerets pump furiously, directing the urine and other body odors forward toward the opponent. They can shoot this stuff a distance of seven body lengths in still water. They open, raise, and spread their claws displaying the lighter undersides of the merus in the meral spread, each still pissing mightily into his opponent's face, neither yet revealing the telltale smell of dominance; it's two males evenly matched and ready to rumble. And as they raise and spread their claws they buzz furiously.

The confrontation escalates. Sonny is the aggressor. He advances on his opponent with claws folded and second antennae lashing. His opponent backs away, claws still raised in the meral spread but antennae erect and immobile. Another inflexion point when a combatant can capitulate by backing out of the arena or tail-flipping away unscathed; this moment passes too. Sonny stops; his opponent advances, seeking to regain ground. They lock claws and like sumo wrestlers each tries to throw the other onto his back. They pull and shove violently, staggering, stumbling, roiling the sand. The situation has become dangerous for both. Now one and then the other, each with a tight grip on his opponent, tries to tail-flip away, a maneuver designed to detach his adversary's claw. Sometimes it works. A claw or some other append-age is torn off or the chitinous armor is punctured. If an eyestalk is ablated the loss is permanent; unlike legs, they can't be regenerated. The eventual loser now telegraphs his impending status by stopping urination. He disen-gages (presuming he can) and retreats.

This battle ends when Sonny's opponent backflips into the night and vanishes. Just prior he had raised his abdomen and bowed to the substrate, his now-single claw extended as if paying homage. Sonny is left victori-ous, clutching a souvenir and also the night's after-fight dinner: his opponent's crusher claw. Ah, the sweet, sweet smell and taste of winning! Nothing beats owning superior urine. He stands rigid and tall like a statue on a plinth, lacking only the burnish of pigeon droppings. He would have huffed, shaken like a wet dog, expiated his sin of indifference with a victorious howl; he would have slathered over the ignominy of his metamorpho-sis, the horror of living his dream. He would have if he could have. Instead, he executes a decapod pirouette as if anticipating applause.

13.

SUMMER HAS ARRIVED BRINGING warmer water. Somewhere above the surface birds sing, flowers bloom, and people complain. Around here at six fathoms the mood is subdued. For millions of lobsters inhabiting the Gulf of Maine a special event will soon occur; actually, sooner than soon. At this very moment it's pounding on Sonny's door to the future. When it appears he will welcome it. . .sort of. Dread it. . .definitely. Dare it, fear it. He feels like a strap-hanger who's fallen onto the subway tracks and through his feet can detect the B train's onrushing reverberations. Sonny might shit his pants were he wearing pants. Instead, he shits where he's standing, on a patch of soft green algae known as mermaid's hair.

Actually, the minor distraction of summer is a relief because he really should try to lose weight prior to the big day or night. In any case, periodic molting is necessary and unavoidable. Sonny needs to shed his existing shell now rigid and shopworn, allowing a growth spurt while the new pliable shell developing underneath expands to accommodate additional tissue. His present shell is restricting him like tight underwear. He sympathizes with that medieval knight grown so fat in his armor he can scarcely breathe.

The Professor is about to give a lecture on the molting process, offering a synopsis of its utility and a description of how it progresses. He chooses a night of full moon, stationing himself in the center a sand patch under the downwelling light. Here he stands as if surrounded by mirrors and vacuously gorging on reflected photons. He is, in his mind, Shakespeare's spineless acolyte, not presenting a boring lecture but staging *A Midsummer Night's Dream* featuring Hermia and Lysander as newly molted lovers. However, he withholds this aspect of oneiric vision for practical reasons: actual lobsters are motivated only by the odors of food and sex. Just former-lies among the local lobster population might attend, and most would not be in their present decapodal situation were they not either philistines or terminally weird. He needs to reconsider the play to make it more relevant and entertaining. At minimum, Lysander must devour the post-molt Hermia and pick his figurative molars with one of her pointy dactyls.

The Professor looks around. Only Sonny and a much smaller formerly have shown up, the other scuttling away when the Professor, forgetting the purpose of their gathering, rushes toward him and shouts, "Put 'em up!"

He turns now to Sonny. "What's your name?"

"Sonny."

"How long have you been here, uh. . .Sonny."

"I'm not wearing a watch."

"Right. Did I ask you to put 'em up when you arrived? Did I ask you to state your name and station?"

"You did."

"Splendid! It's marvelous when protocol has been observed. Now, why are you here?"

"For your lecture on molting."

The professor hopes to hide his perplexity by appearing thoughtful. He touches the dactyl of a walking leg to an eyestalk, then scratches his statocysts one after the other; that is, the section of shell overlying them.

Never mind, he's back. He moves to the center of the sand patch illuminated by flickering moonlight. He holds up his right claw (which happens to be the crusher) as if stilling a restless audience, turning clockwise in a slow circle until once again facing Sonny. The academic life had never replaced his secret dream of being a thespian, to stand under bright theater lights absorbing their warmth, waving and bowing to adoring fans waiting with bated breath to hear him speak his lines, or perhaps bait breath is more apropos in these surroundings. However, the yearning to project his voice resonating with the rustic melodrama of timeless poetry is not to be. And so, the lecture begins.

The Professor opens by explaining a lobster shell's function. The inside of a lobster, he says, is soft, squishy, has the consistency of jelly, and is highly vulnerable. It needs protection from dangers without; it demands physical support from the rigid external shell, which secures the delicate fluids and organs within and holds them in place. In contrast, a vertebrate's supporting structure is internal, a scaffold of bones and cartilage from which the organs hang and through which the life-giving fluids circulate. Instead of chitinous armor, many vertebrates are encased in easily punctured layers of exposed skin, not an especially efficient development considering how the upper world is rife with sharp objects. The Professor offers a quote about molting from Frances Hobart Herrick's 1911 monograph on the American lobster: "Molting is an incident and expression of growth. The crustacean does not 'grow by molting,' as is sometimes said, but it molts because it has grown." The Professor then describes how a lobster's growth after the final metamorphosis is indeterminate, meaning it doesn't terminate but continues throughout life, although the rate tapers off with age. Humans, in contrast, express determinate growth, attaining maximum length (being bipeds, humans call this "height") at maturity. There you have it, the elements of growth succinctly circumscribed.

Molting — also called ecdysis — proceeds in a predictable sequence of moves, and a misstep at any point is potentially life-threatening. A single maneuver executed improperly can leave the animal stuck in the old shell to suffocate. However, the Professor continues, let us not look backward while thinking morbid thoughts. Instead, we should march forward into the promising post-molt future that awaits us all.

Sonny has taken the Professor's previous lectures seriously. When he transitioned it was into an adult lobster's body, "coming out on the other side" (as formerlies term their metamorphosis) without experiencing the vicissitudes of the many molts a normal lobster endures. Molting frequency declines with age. A lobster molts about nine times during its first year of life and about twenty-five times between hatching and sexual maturity at age five or six years, then perhaps annually. Having reached twenty-five pounds and twenty inches in length, growth slows, and intervals between molts might extend several years.

There is the physical unpleasantness of the procedure itself to consider, the Professor emphasizes, but also such social consequences as how it affects agonism and the temporary loss of dominance. A molted male will be bigger immediately afterward and more imposing, but size as a measure of status can be illusory. Actually, he will have gone from muscular Charles Atlas preening on the beach to puny weakling likely to get sand kicked in his face by bullies. He must avoid confrontation until his shell hardens and his muscles develop and regain strength.

Sonny is told he will lose his appetite and not eat for several days immediately prior to ecdysis. This is an instinctive device helping his tissues shrink to make shedding the shell easier. The combination of fasting and hormonal intervention will reduce his muscle mass thirty to sixty percent. Much of this loss will be in the claws, which are particularly difficult to extract from the old shell, akin to peeling off skin-tight gloves. He also will shun food during the first days post-molt, and when he does eat the diet will consist predominantly of soft foods until the crusher and cutter claws regain their hard surfaces and rigid teeth and the muscles that power them develop adequately.

Recovery is prolonged. The new shell takes six to eight weeks to harden completely, and return to full physical and physiological condition takes about three months. But he should not be distressed. A sun shines brightly on the horizon (metaphorically speaking). Having discarded its constricting shell the newly molted lobster instantly extends its body length by roughly fifteen percent and expands fifty percent in volume.

Only a few days post-lecture Sonny acquires a pre-molt attitude. He's more active, buzzing here and there looking frantically for a proper shelter site in which to hole up and molt. He's more irritable than usual, hair-triggered you might say, unpredictable as an errant axe head ripe for departing its handle. He's showing evidence of displacement activity, taking out his frustrations by crushing mussels into powder with execrable force, not from hunger but just for the helluva it. He rips apart polychaetes and tosses aside the remnants like shredded paper, pulverizes entire colonies of sea squirts to unrecognizable mush. What a temper!

Sonny, you see, is on steroids, specifically, ecdysteroids such as the molting hormone ecdysone, which right now is raging through his hemolymph as molting draws near. And do not discount a certain peptide, crustacean hyperglycemic hormone, which also is peaking and promotes aggression. He's become a crustacean poster boy of predacity, a lobsterly emulation of The Hulk. He tramps forcefully here and there on this particular moonless night jamming the pointed dactyls of his last two pairs of walking legs deep into the substrate and angrily disregarding one of their normal functions, which is to lightly probe the benthos for sensory hints of hidden prey. We also know of several battles recently instigated and won. He strides thick and heavy-clawed across the stony seascape oblivious to any danger. He seeks — no, he demands and deserves — the perfect shelter in which to cloister himself for the imminent ordeal, not just the event but afterward when he must endure that extended period of vulnerability.

Ah, here it is! He pokes a tentative second antenna through the doorway where another antenna touches his. He rushes inside, grapples with the resident, and quickly evicts him. The other lobster back-flips into the darkness minus a walking leg. The dude was a palooka. That's Sonny in pre-molt mode: one kick-telson decapod and a mean motor scooter.

The moment arrives like an icy Arctic current. He edges away from the shelter entrance, no longer guarding it with the barrage of his formidable claws. His forestomach seems unusually active, and he's belching up bits of food plus some sand and other undigestible debris. Dyspepsia? Gastroesophageal reflux disease? Neither is likely. The lobster esophagus is frightfully short. Furthermore, there is no chance that a lobster, no matter how hungry, bolts its food. Therefore, dyspepsia is doubtfully ever an issue. As Frances Hobart Herrick wrote in 1911, "The higher Crustacea are the only animals which grind the food after it reaches the stomach as well as before it enters the mouth." Food is repeatedly masticated and swallowed, burped up, then chewed and swallowed again. The process goes on for hours after a meal. That's *really* chewing your food adequately. His present feeling of unpleasantness is apt to be associated with this method of digestion: barf a little into your mouthparts, chew the vomit, then swallow it again, similar to a cow chewing a cud. Admittedly, not GERD exactly or cud-chewing either, but something. . . .similar. Christ, he feels awful.

An hour before onset of these symptoms he started rapidly swallowing seawater and will continue doing so through the first two hours post-molt. Over this time approximately ninety percent of the seawater ingested will have joined the hemolymph, coinciding with his impending weight gain. Hardly an embarrassing situation; it's only "water weight." During the interval between molts excess water is replaced gradually with new tissues and in this way the lobster "grows into" its replacement shell. The amount of water ingested equals that absorbed by the tissues while ecdysis progresses, indicating that the newly swallowed seawater has joined the hemolymph and become part of the

77

"bloodstream." Taking in so much liquid this suddenly distends the gut, helping loosen the carapace from its underlying membranes and enabling that part of the shell to be released more easily.

The molt begins with separation of the front part of the body from the abdomen, jackknifing Sonny's torso and leaving him momentarily poised on the substrate balancing on the edge of his telson and tips of his claws. Then the membrane underneath this joint ruptures, the legs begin pulling free, and except for the statocysts his shell slips off in a single piece, like a jumpsuit. The entire molting process usually takes only a few minutes. As mentioned, each maneuver is critical. If the sequence does not proceed smoothly and the animal becomes stuck, the result could be fatal.

Think our boy felt queasy before molting? Best not to dwell on it, he tells himself. Not just the shell in all its detail is consigned to the trash heap. With it go most of the tendons, setae, and the digestive and reproductive systems. These are all regrown with every molt. The legs are extracted along with the mouthparts, gills, antennae and antennules, even the eyestalks and swimmerets. Pulling out the claws without damaging them is especially difficult. It requires compressing the muscle tissue, shrinking it away from the interior shell surfaces and then drawing out each reduced, naked appendage through the narrow opening at its base where the two sections of the claw attach to the adjoining leg segment (the carpus), a hole having a diameter less than one-fourth the breadth of the claws at their widest.

Some vital minerals already have been extracted during the molting process and translocated to the hemolymph for deposition in the new shell. To supplement these Sonny now turns to the trash heap and munches on his old shell, regaining from its remnants some of the lost calcium carbonate and other minerals to now blend with his burgeoning new chitin and help stiffen it.

The molt has been completed without a hitch or glitch. Sonny collapses, exhausted. He's hollowed out, sucked dry, barely managing to stand on his hardening pins despite water's buoyancy. This must be how a human woman feels after giving birth. His agonism-promoting, gonad-busting hormones have declined abruptly, and with them went the confidence of a dominant lobster. He has suddenly become a quivering subaltern producing frequent buzzes. Could these be the analog of moans and groans? Is Sonny experiencing a moment of self-pity? If so, who could blame him? He's just survived a tortuous tumultuous tainture of horrific hormonal hammering. As mentioned, the new shell will not harden completely for months, and during this interregnum he won't feel like fighting. The urge, when next it visits, will require starting over, conquering his antagonists sequentially until again attaining the pinnacle and becoming Thunder Claw (*Tonitrus Unguibus*)!

It occurs to Sonny that equating molting with rebirth is illusory, another lie. Ha! Shed everything and return a changed lobster? The ship of Theseus paradox: after losing and replacing nearly every part of your physical self, are you still you? I've disappeared and been reconstituted both within and without, he thinks, and still I can't discern if I ever was me. Maybe this undersea world is nothing but a boundless sensory deprivation tank and I'm its sallow hallucination. If so, evolution has blundered into a cul-de-sac. There surely must be more, possibly less. Christ, and he can't even shout his frustration.

Reality is the mask we wear to hide the inchoateness and acedia of our continuing metamorphoses. Inside that pristine new shell sloshes a larger but diluted Sonny, not a stronger, tougher one. Not yet. Right now, Sonny feels like a timorous trembling tardigrade. Considering tardigrades are microscopic, that's very small indeed. Macroscopically, he's a rapidly evaporating shadow of his former self and feeling about. . .this. . .big.

14.

PHILIP MARLOWE, THE PROTAGONIST in Raymond Chandler's novel *Killer in the Rain*, encounters a blonde with black eyes. Not an ordinary blonde, Marlowe tells us, but a blonde who could inspire a bishop to kick a hole in a stained-glass window. We might infer from Marlowe's vivid description some biological clues. First, this is a blonde on the prowl; second, despite his cloistered celibacy the bishop has recognized and understood her lusty signals.

Switching now to an analogous scene in which the characters are crustaceans, we might begin by stating confidently that lobster society is crassly chauvinistic. Males sometimes attack females, on occasion even killing and eating them. However, when it comes to choosing a mate, it's female choice. A female experiencing the lobsterly equivalent of estrus — an urge to mate but folded into a need to molt first (think getting naked) — it's she who goes looking for a suitable partner, putatively a dominant male, and boldly enters his shelter. This act, the consequent of her choice, is more hopeful than confirmed. It announces, at this point, only her availability. However, it doesn't guarantee the male's acceptance. Certain conditions must be met before consummation.

The two start pissing into each other's face, the female

more vigorously. If she fails to release her copious share the male might attack her, perhaps suspecting she could be a he-lobster challenging his ownership of the shelter. An unknown component of female urine lessens male aggression, but evidently delivering it in bulk helps her cause. Once inside the dark, dangerous den of the cave bear she further introduces herself haptically through antennal contact, and by ongoing chemical communication through her urine she confirms her sexual status and availability. He reciprocates, announcing his own status and availability through the maleness of his urine and by touching her with his antennae. In other words, he smells, tastes, feels her, and then decides whether to let her stay or toss her out on her telson. Sure, he has been her choice, but the nuances extend deeper.

It's late in the molting season. Sonny has gone through his first molt and recovered. Now that he's again a dominant lobster, he wonders when a chitinous siren might appear on his doorstep vibrating with a hushed appetency and the scurrilous hope of playing antennal patty-cake. He won't wait long. While relaxing inside his shelter after a hearty meal of blue mussels and polychaetes, Sonny experiences just such a situation. An adult premolt female of the crustacean persuasion with thoughts of sex jangling in her fifteen separate ganglion clusters — a lobster's substitute for a brain — pushes boldly into his living room/kitchen/bedroom/privy. She too is a black-eyed blonde, a blonde to reverse a battery's polarity, snarl an anchor line, twist a bow cleat ninety degrees. She's flashing a razored decapodal face and pumping along on seven-segmented getaway sticks times eight (despite having ten "legs," lobsters don't walk on their claws). She's a formerly and lets him know telepathically that she's a golden lobster, a choice rarity. Then again, she could have said she was red, white, or blue; lobsters are colorblind. Even in that dimness the smoothness of her walking legs distresses Sonny's faceted vision. If truly a blonde lobster then she, like him, is a genetic anomaly, one in thirty million, and here she stands before him subtly wiggling her tail fan and trying to manufacture a come-hither stare. Sadly, this last semiotic sign has been wasted in the surrounding darkness. Still, the twenty-seven thousand miniature lenses of Sonny's compound eyes (of the two eyes combined) have become occluded. Could be that in lobster love chemistry trumps vision.

She pushes inside, *sui generis* and not just because of her pigmentation, but importunate, an instant disturbance, a fracture in the benthic containment. She tramps saucily around his personal space, tapping antennae on every surface including him, as if conducting a prospective home-buyer's assessment and deciding if the contents meet her standards. She pictures Sonny as a hog to be tied and wonders why these subterranean dumps never have a sound system. She's a lively assortment of spineless insistence and spiny persistence. All in all, she's one helluva hot invertebrate, and she's intent on shredding any masculine resistance by Sonny — that is, his hubris — like a coconut grater. Out of horniness he capitulates to the vicissitudes of letting her to stay and tell her story, evidently a mandatory prelude to undersea boogie-woogie.

She has picked up a little knowledge of folk genetics and knows that progeny of two recessives will likely be born with certain inevitable phenotypes matching those of the parents: two blue-eyed humans will produce only blue-eyed offspring. Seeing how they both are golden, a color deviating from the norm and a recessive trait, the possibility of achieving a pedestrian form of dominance over the ordinary camouflage-green members of their species excites her. Here is a chance to jointly parent a pure Aryan race of lobsters defined by yellow-pigmented chitin. He yawns at this disquisition, or tries to, but that maneuver doesn't work underwater through three pairs of aquatically adapted mouthparts. He swallows hard instead and explains that their fellow lobsters can't perceive colors and won't notice, that a lobster's visual world is black and white splashed over and numbed by infinite shades of gray. Clearly a social climber, she ignores him.

And so he asks what he really should have asked from the start, the history of her metamorphosis. This is every formerly's favorite story, seeing how it's the biggest event of their lives, and she eagerly pours out hers. At age nineteen with a high school diploma she had gone to work in the office of a large corporation. She was pretty, maybe not Marlowe's stunner, but a natural blonde with a tasty figure. Her job was entry-level. She ran errands, made endless photocopies, and delivered coffee and mail to a hive of cubicles while trying to evade the sticky hands of their mostly male occupants. It was like navigating through an octopus colony. Even the big boss, whose dry cleaning she delivered and retrieved, had groped her.

Things were no better at home, where she shared a flat with her divorced mother, an office worker in a different part of the city who came home drunk when she came home at all, and was a potty-mouth chain-smoker with brown teeth. "Why aren't you engaged yet?" It was the question her mother asked relentlessly. "Maybe you don't put out enough. Take my advice, that's what you gotta do to get a husband. Choose some stiff who ain't used to steady pussy. Them's the ones you can snag easiest." Then the inevitable argument. "Yeah, that's worked real good for you, Mom. You're a great example. Advice from a woman who sees life upside-down from flat on her back."

One day a photo caught her eye. It was on the front page of a newspaper in her mail cart and accompanied by a story of a "blonde" lobster donated to the local public aquarium by the lobstermen who had trapped it. The animal is female and a rich golden color. Such specimens are exceedingly rare, the article said, one in many millions. This one is also larger than most, about five pounds. A notch in her tail put there by an unknown lobsterman indicates she has been captured before when berried. It signifies a demonstrated breeder that must be released. She will be held at the aquarium until suitable press coverage could be arranged for her repatriation to the capture site. Meanwhile, visitors are welcome to view her.

Why not? she thought. That Saturday morning she took a bus to the aquarium, a drab gray building at the end of the city pier operated by a consortium of marine science affiliates and administered by Downeast University. The structure was single-level, the size of a Midwestern tract house. A poster at the entrance told the building's history. Originally built by a fishermen's cooperative as a meeting place and storage area for traps, nets, oars, and other gear, it had fallen into disrepair and later became a small public aquarium and education center.

The lobster exhibit was easy to find: it was the one with a crowd around it, maybe ten or fifteen people leaning in or elbowing to the front for a better view. The creature was indeed spectacular, considerably bigger than lobsters featured live at seafood restaurants — perhaps four times their size — and a vibrant golden color.

There were oohs and aahs mixed with the expected jokes of how she might taste if boiled, cracked open, and slathered with melted lemon-butter.

The aquarium's curator, a young man in his mid-twenties, sidled up to her. He told her he could give her a better look and led her behind the scenes where he temporarily shut off the flow of seawater into the exhibit. With the surface stilled they could look directly down through the pristine water and observe the lobster in full dorsal view.

It was possibly the most beautiful thing she had ever seen, and she unconsciously emitted a little squeal of pleasure. He asked for her phone number and invited her to accompany him, along with the press and lobstermen who had donated it, when a date had been picked for its release back into the Gulf of Maine. She accepted enthusiastically. But the golden lobster now had her entranced. She started spending most of her free time at the aquarium, staring at it, watching as it slowly drew its antennules through its third maxillipeds to clean them and keep the sensory receptor cells unobstructed. The curator explained this behavior to her, along with other tidbits of lobster biology and behavior whenever he entered the public area and noticed her bent over in front of the display, nose to the glass. At night, while she sat before the mirror brushing her hair, she compared its color with the lobster's. They were nearly a perfect match, and she wondered if the same might be true underwater.

She became obsessed with the blonde lobster, scarcely able to think about anything else, so fixated that it appeared in her dreams, and when awake the scene around transformed into a phantasmagoria of pareidolia: she saw ghostly images of blonde lobsters everywhere.

They appeared fleetingly on advertising signs; they embellished the mannequins in department store windows and even graced for a nanosecond the yellow winter coat worn by a woman standing at an intersection. She rearranged her wardrobe, choosing to wear mainly yellow colors, speculating whether after her many visits the lobster recognized her.

The day of its release arrived with a fierce onshore wind blowing curtains sleet. She met the curator at the aquarium entrance. Inside, he provided a full set of oilskins and boots, and having pulled them on over her own clothes she accompanied him out a back door to the edge of the pier where a lobster boat was tied, and its owner and his sternman, also in full oilskins, waited on standby. She and the curator climbed aboard, and soon a reporter and cameraman from a local TV news station showed up. They would produce a short clip to be aired on the evening news. With them was the editor of the aquarium's monthly newsletter, who also carried a camera and intended to write a feature story for the membership.

The lobster had been transferred to the boat's live well. They shoved off, bow hammering into the disturbed sea. Frothy surfactants torn from the faces of the waves melted into the spindrift to be mixed with sleet and snow. Visibility was reduced to a few feet. After motoring nearly an hour, the skipper navigating by waypoints on his GPS monitor, they slowed and stopped. "This heah's the spot we was trappin," he said. "You'd wanted to take this-heah lobstah home, ayuh. No need to drap iron. She'll know the place soon's she hits bottom."

With the camera rolling the curator hiked up his sleeves and lifted out the lobster waving its antennae and legs. "Say goodbye to the people," said the curator, smiling at the camera. At that instant her knees gave way, and she lurched toward the lobster, arm out, intending to touch it. Startled, the curator turned aside, and she toppled over the low gunnel, sinking instantly. She never knew, of course, how frantically those aboard tried to find her, but she was never in sight. With visibility nearly zero, the sea near freezing, the wind and waves carrying her away from them, she might survive twenty minutes even with her head above water. The situation was hopeless. The captain radioed the Coast Guard, gave their position, stood by for two hours, and turned for home.

She mentions to Sonny that the curator guy was a cutie and had some weird, nowhere kind of education, like, maybe marine biology. Her mom might have approved, except for his job, of course, which mostly seemed to be feeding fish to other fish. What kind of career path is that? Better if he was a banker or accountant or maybe in real estate. Oh well. Doesn't matter now.

15.

"So, THAT'S IT," SHE says to Sonny. "Next I know I'm
that lobster. What the hell, at least I'm alive. I think
about Mom and the scene she must've made. 'Oh my
darling daughter, the love of my life, how will I live without her? Will I get any insurance money?'" She raises
a walking leg to her mouthparts and makes a drinking
motion. "'Bartender, another double scotch, and would
you be a sweetheart and empty the ashtray? By the way,
you're quite a handsome young man. You should have
met my daughter, you'd have been perfect together.' Sly
little chuckle, batting of eyelashes. 'Naturally, bartender,
she took after me. People used to think we were sisters.
Would you be a sweetheart again and light my cigarette?'
Ah, dear old Mombo. Jesus, what a skank. Oops, mind
turning your back? I'm feeling the urge to slip into something more comfortable. It's personal."

She's referring to a new shell, of course. And Sonny
is in for a surprise. A newly molted female gives off an
enticing perfume filling the male's shelter with prom-
ises of sex he finds irresistible. To get re-acquainted
afterward they romantically piss in each other's faces.
Newly molted, her carapace is glabrous and unsullied
by epibionts. It's emitting sweet pungent smelly-smells

of amino acids. Truly, the way to a male lobster's heart is via his three stomachs and gastric mill. Oh my! Could he be thinking. . . .He congratulates her on the delicious sleekness of her enticingly soft, digestible shell, remarks on how smooth and svelte she looks despite missing a goodly pair of *poitrines*, compliments that leave her nervous, shaking in her new chitins. He's been hanging out with the Professor recently and begun talking like him. He projects his best lobsterly leer and says, "You look fetching, my dear, so comestible and tasty in your new dress; that is, undressed and all dressed up like a dropsied tick. I'm slightly nauseous from that molting performance (sorry, I peeked), although still feeling a tetch cannibalistic. That's lobster love, I suppose. Want to hold crusher claws? Aw shit, sorry, didn't mean to lunge at you. Unsteady on the ol' pins, huh? Don't try standing until that new shell hardens some, heh, heh." He takes a bite or two of her old shell discarded nearby. The flavor reminds him of McDonald's fries hot from the grease but with a distinctly fishy aftertaste. She watches furtively and shudders, thinking the act piranhic, but it's innocent: he's only hoping to gain a hit of calcium carbonate to stiffen a strategic part of his own anatomy.

Shivering a little, she retreats deeper into the shelter. He drops her shell and follows, saying, "I find you delectably dialectical, me deeah, fah a lobstah, as we Downeastahs say. I mean, especially one who used to be human. Yes indeed, you smell deliciosus." Thus inspired he puts on the cool-daddy decapod strut, fluttering the maxillipeds of his mouthparts (the analogue of licking his lips), rapidly flicking the antennules (like sniffing her all over), and standing tall on the tips of his walking legs. Gustation and sex have blended seamlessly until everything is food. The setae of his antennules and walking legs have been alerted by the scrumptious amino acids and complex carbohydrates sloughing off her new shell, and by the lipidy flavor of her exhalations.

The feeling of having become a seafood taco stuffed with desirable food groups sends her into jerks and shivers of insecurity that he misinterprets as lust for him. He now peers at her goggle-eyed, eyestalks more twisted than a mountain road. He tries to spit out a natty cantrip, but nothing comes to mind (no surprise here), so instead he performs a dainty shuffle (two steps to the left, two to the right), stirring the water and bringing more of her scent closer to the setae of his antennules, anything to stoke the fever and supersize that pheromone high. Oh boy! He's facing her, fanning the swimmerets under his abdomen rapidly and drawing water toward himself the better to sniff it faster, then pushing it out the shelter entrance. Antennules are flicking in overdrive.

The scene is ripe for a submarine epithalamium echoing those ancient Greek poems written for brides on their way to the marital chamber, except there's nobody but them. He might buzz her carapace in free verse but decides to let the moment pass. Maybe a different time, a different lobster. He strokes her with his second antennae, gaining another chemosensory rush through the setae of the antennules, not to mention via some of the setae in his knees, like, all his knees. She reciprocates by stroking him with her second antennae and finally feels her own blast of concupiscence. They lie down on their ventrums side by side. After a half-hour, or thereabouts, he drapes a fifth walking leg across her and gently rolls her onto her back. She doesn't resist and helps by extending and crossing her claws to shift them out of the way.

Head to head, mouthparts locked in full segmented chumble and everything else in bewildered arthropod entanglement, he stands and mounts her, balancing himself on the tips of his claws and walking legs. God now enforces a universal dictum: these might be soulless invertebrates, but still they do it missionary style. "Oh hold me tight against your cold, spineless body," she buzzes.

Is this really the Book of Love or just the Cliff Notes? Sonny is clueless. She half-heartedly offers the canard about it being her first time, blowing off any significance of previous matings. Those episodes had been consummated prior to her sexual maturation and the sperm inserted inside her subsequently discarded with the old shell and associated paraphernalia at her next molt. Females that mate while immature are usually a single molt away from sexual maturity. In other words, she explains, those encounters don't count, they were just "practice" for the real event, which she claims is fulminating momentarily. As he flips her over she murmurs, "Fecundate me you decapodal hunk, but please be gentle. I've never carried embryos before and don't believe I could stand squeezing out more than four or five thousand eggs after my first real spin around the dance floor."

You sly slut, he's thinking, handing me this mangled wreck of equivocation, this guilty dénouement trailing after departed humanhood. But then, what did I expect from a blind date in the dark at ten fathoms? Take a look at your surroundings, pilgrim. This is how it is, the floor of the Gulf of Maine as sleazy pickup bar. So, grind that gastric mill in frustration all you want, but get used to regurgitating the grit. Lift up thine compound eyes and watch the marine snow spin and gyrate into strings of hooker-beads. And the fuzzy stuff on the curtains standing in for fake felt? Turf algae sliming the rocks, be careful where you step.

From here it gets real. He senses the lamb of his innocence being driven over the horizon, waggling its ass-end toward enlightenment as it vanishes. Surely, there's more. She buzzes a message about something poking her in repetitious thrusts. Such has lobster foreplay reach its nadir. He inserts his modified first swimmerets into her seminal receptacles and shoots out spermatophores. These conveniently wrapped packages of sperm will be stored internally until she uses them to later fertilize her eggs, which will occur externally as she extrudes and cements them to her swimmerets to develop into embryos. The procedure is akin to handing your date a suitcase stuffed with sperm while seeing her off at the train station. And now for the real grins and giggles. According to bumper stickers in Oklahoma, a typical bull rider at the rodeo lasts eight seconds; around these parts a stud lobster hangs in a full minute, more or less.

"Oh my gawd," she buzzes, "ride me, cowboy!" She clutches him in a writhing and clearly aural crepitation of stiffening leg joints (her new shell is hardening). A passerby might wonder what the sea anemones attached to the walls and ceiling are thinking. The act culminates in a blurted epenthesis, a draw-r-ing out of buzz-z-zing, and if he'd possessed a backbone she would have razored its knuckles from end to end like keys of xylophone. Goodness, such parabiotic joy.

Her buzz suddenly corrades to a burble. "Hot damn, that was tide-turning majorly hellacious! Was it good for you too?" Then she adds, "Those first swimmerets of yours are quite some woodies, or rockies, I should probably say, considering they're calcified. Anyhow, you jammed 'em to me right-good. What's that you're buzz-ing? How long 'til you see your chilluns?" (Retention time of the developing eggs until hatching ordinarily takes nine months to nearly a year. That's how long.)

Maybe he already knows he's free to ghost having completed the stick and run, the old slap and tickle. She says, "Maybe we'll be in the same neighborhood after a few of the little frackers survive to the fourth stage, drop from the water column to the benthos, and take their first baby steps. But let's not get too eager about exchanging future itineraries. For shit's sake, I might still be here in the Gulf of Maine long after you've traipsed off to Long Island Sound, or thereabouts, in search of some off-colored paisley bitch of your dreams. Hey boy, I've been hanging around your squalor more'n a week. You really need to take out the trash. Just look at the entryway: crushed mussel shells and half-eaten polychaetes everywhere, can't set down a dactyl without stepping on a squishy lump of sea squirt tunic or tripping over crushed crab shells. . .my old shell moldering in the corner and stinking up the place. Well, gotta go gestate. Move your sorry telson aside, I'm outta here. Smell and taste you around someday."

This female has a permanent attitude, but just wait. She's not yet berried. Her aggression and moxie will only increase once she's carrying developing embryos under-neath her abdomen. Berried female lobsters turn witchy, becoming true termagants, and fights between them are exceptionally ferocious. Stay out of her way.

She leaves the shelter abruptly. She eye-stalks out, you might say, striding into the turbid dawn on four snappy new pairs of walking legs. Lobster trysts aren't guaranteed to end joyfully. Sonny recalls a discussion with the Professor on the subject of lobster love. "There's no such thing," the Professor had said. "There's only lobster lust. I mean, open your compound eyes, we're invertebrates for chrissakes!" Sonny hopes another female won't visit soon. Some males are visited as many as fifty times in single season. Please, not now. He's exhausted and short of spermatophores. He needs to restock his ammunition. He needs an intermission from intromission.

16.

ICY WATER ARISING IN the Gulf of St. Lawrence and carried by the Nova Scotia Current slides southwest through the Cabot Strait and crosses the Scotian Shelf. It rounds peninsular Nova Scotia at Cape Sable and roars northeast into the tube-shaped, dead-end Bay of Fundy. Return flow out of this cul-de-sac enters the western Gulf of Maine and splits into the Gulf of Maine Gyre, a counterclockwise current that loops back into the Bay of Fundy, and another, more expansive counterclockwise current deflected south by Maine's coast until dividing near Cape Cod. Part of it then continues south around the Cape into the Atlantic. The other part flows east into the Atlantic, forming a counterclockwise current encircling Georges Bank.

Has this brief disquisition been boring? Not at all! Snap to! Excavate y'all some education and munch down on it! Get your lazy asses on the Internet and whistle up a map of ocean currents in the Gulf of Maine. How hard can it be? My, my, nobody wants to work at learning these days. It's disgraceful. Just show me the video then I won't have to think, okay? Am I right? Ah hell, forget it. Stop reading this and go to the kitchen, pop some corn, maybe snap on the teevee when you come back. You're probably wondering what this synopsis of the Gulf of Maine's regional oceanography — distilled into a measly five sentences — has to do with Sonny. Well, every-damn-thing if you're paying attention.

Sonny has ignored the Professor's advice about moving east of Suramoh Island and wintering in deeper, warmer water instead of freezing his telson inshore. He chooses a rocky area a couple of miles from the island in barely four fathoms, although luckily finding a secure crevice in which to sequester for the months ahead. Still, it's shallow enough to make him rock and reel with the storm surges overhead. For entertainment he watches shredded, shadowy strands of kelp drift past, ripped apart by the waves. During bitter winter nights he pictures ice blanketing the intertidal boulders at Suramoh, blistering the exposed rockweed and crusting the tidepools. His energy sapped, he has recently offered feeble but adequate resistance to repel another lobster equally cold-compromised who had envied his crevice and made a half-hearted attempt at eviction.

At dawn one morning he creeps from the shelter and looks up, noticing that the light filtering through the surface is an unsettled gray. There passes a fleeting anamnesis when suddenly this view from underneath becomes a similitude of Maine's querulous wintery sky. He's homesick, but for what? The chicken farm? Hardly. The land? No. The land would seem more useful if the water vapor overlying it condensed fully and changed phase. Then creatures willing and able to mostly dispense with gravity could float in it. How strange, he thinks, to be reasoning from a lobster's viewpoint.

He dozes through most of the hours in numbed torpor, claws side by side at his doorway forming the usual barrage. The sea around him is thirty-three degrees Fahrenheit, sometimes slipping into the high twenties, although never congealing into ice because salt lowers the freezing point of water. He has little motivation to eat, and his energy reserves of glycogen and lipids are becoming depleted. Actually, he can last all winter without food, but barely, and spring would find him too weak to sustain the rigors of dominance, molting, and mating. He really should venture out and rustle up some grub, but at the moment he's snipping epibionts from the walls and low ceiling of the crevice and from his own carapace and pushing them slowly into his mouthparts. He seems to be sleepwalking, and in effect he is.

The motions Sonny is experiencing are programmed and repetitive. His taste receptors in hesitant, cold-addled communion with nerve cells inside his shell, drive the monotonous grasping of edible items by pincers of the first two pairs of walking legs and direct them to the mouthparts. And while he trips along on autopilot, he dreams. Even these dream images seem to arrive and depart in slow motion, as if standing at his entrance in bleak sadness awaiting their turns.

During sleep, dreams appear as occultations between your separated selves, one awake, the other not. They resketch your familiar outline, the image you recognize as you, by switching on the mind's autonomic catoptrics, bending and distorting the margins, painting in the shadows, reimagining your voice while adjusting its timbre. Dreams exhume repellent corpses of old fears; hence, the subconscious disquiet that sometimes persists long after the episode is forgotten.

He dreams of a dark-skinned girl from a long-ago music video, now a strangely lobsterized, lobstersized human — a crustacean cutie, a decapod dolly. There's memory of background music, but only a memory of the memory, nothing of the music itself. Here she is, the lobster-girl, directly before him, looking at him with black buggy eyes. A disembodied male voice somewhere out of sight talks jive. . . .

"Wake up, lobster-boy! Darksome lady at the doorstep. Lithe, white teeth. Don't shade me, son, I know you care deeply 'bout culture. Hokay, I'll kickstart this here roadshow. We off! Hey girl, put a shimmy in that there buzz, know what I'm sayin'? Shake it around a teensie bit, try'na 'rouse the froze-ass citizens o' this god-fo'saken hellhole. Shake and toddle atop them skinny legs, oh yes! Slip y'all's pointy toes into *chaussures à talons hauts* and go struttin', tippy-dactyl'n through the sea squirts. Lookie all them feet! Sugar, you gonna need you more'n one pair, thass right. What we want is laughter lubricated by chemical stimulation and music, but none o' that down here, nossir. Nobody (or nothin') laughs 'cause ain't nothin' funny, catch my drift? No disco lights. In fact, barely any light at all. Music? Listen close and say if you feelin' a dance-beat. Ha! Only snaps, crackles, and pops; bleeps and crunch o' mastication. Sense that? We lobster-people cain't hear jack-shit, a'course, but at least wake up them mechanosensory setae coverin' y'all's carapace and them other organs too on y'all's legs, antennules, antennae, claws, and mouthparts. Try'na tune in the roller derby collisions o' displacin' particles bumpin' shoulders, construction clank and screech o' predators buildin' 'em a subsea bricolage out'n fish bones and clam shells and other after-dinner inedibles, a shiny new altar fo' worshippin' the taste and smell o' fear. Dream, muthafuckas, dream."

17.

THEY HAD BEEN SHELTERING in the same vicinity, Sonny, the Professor, and Day Tripper, bumping into each other more than usual. It's springtime, and the Professor is feeling springy. He dispatches an announcement to all formerlies who might be within telepathic receiving distance that he intends to hold a lecture on pain the following night during a full moon. The subject, he says, will be of interest to all formerlies, considering that they now are lobsters and at risk of being captured by humans and boiled alive. Is the process painful? Do the victims suffer? These questions are squarely at the intersection of science and philosophy.

He says that his lecture will take place here, on this very patch of sand. The flat slab of schist near its center will be his lectern. You could also call it, he adds with a soggy sniggle, his "decapodium." Sonny sniggles too when receiving the message, but Day Tripper's communicative pipeline remains silent as a silent spring. Day Tripper has issues with recondite matters, or subtleties of any sort. No worries. With nothing better to do, his disruptive self is certain to appear, playing class clown and deliberately pissing off the Professor.

Under different circumstances we might begin by

saying the day dawned bright and cloudless, but under the ocean where this story takes place it's usually dark and always cloudless. The actual setting is the bottom of the Gulf of Maine illuminated by a few tremulous, lonely photons struggling through several fathoms of really dirty water.

Then day dissolves into night. It's too dark to discern much of anything even at plenilune, but with a little effort the Professor can be imagined striding to his decapodium and looking left and right then straight ahead at his audience of two. "Greetings, seekers of knowledge," he says sarcastically. "The subject of tonight's lecture is pain: what it is, how it happens, and whether it can be perceived by spineless invertebrates such as ourselves. I realize the redundancy of my comment about 'spineless invertebrates,' but dull subjects are often made enjoyable by a little humor." We presume the Professor hesitates, awaiting an appreciative response, but continues when receiving no acknowledgment.

Day Tripper says, "Oy Prof, where's the pole dancers? Me and Thunder Claw, we're here for the action. Wouldn't that be a gas? A chix lobster sliding up and down a pole massaging her swimmerets? Hot *damn*!"

Although prepared for disruption, the Professor is nonetheless startled. "What or who is Thunder Claw?"

"Sonny here. My homie. I give him that name a while back. See the size of the crusher mitt on this crustacean? Damn-*nation*!

The Professor sighs in a lobsterly manner and regroups. "Okay, the opening pages of Stephen King's novel *The Drawing of the Three* finds the protagonist, Roland, last of the gunslingers, wet and shivering on a cobble beach trying to recover from a near-death experience. As he catches his breath he's approached by a 'lobstrosity.' The creature emerges from the waves, armored and segmented, about four feet long and a foot tall. It weighs maybe seventy pounds and vaguely resembles a lobster or scorpion. Roland notices that it's equipped with two powerful claws and a beak for a mouth; it seems bold and passively aggressive. Before he can reach for his pistols the creature rips into the boot on his right foot and bites off his big toe.

"While approaching Roland but still some distance away it had paused intermittently, looked up at him with stalked eyes and claws spread threateningly, and emitted a series of plaintive vocalizations with lilting endings, as if asking questions. 'Did-a-chick?' it says, seeming to imply, 'Won't you help me? Can't you see how distraught I've become?' While Roland is bent down feeling the bloody space left by his missing toe the creature promptly chomps off the index and middle fingers of his right hand. 'Dum-a-chum? Dad-a-cham? Ded-a-check?' Jesus Christ, it bites off his trigger finger! Nearly as disturbing to a gun-slinger like Roland, his ammo has taken a heavy soaking while he rolled in the surf attempting to gain footing and clamor ashore. A hero's first duty is to keep his powder dry. Sure enough, he aims at the encroaching menace and three times pulls the trigger left-handed. *Click, click,* and *click*. Our hero is in trouble. 'Dod-a-chock?'

"Meanwhile, his interlocutor continues to display its claws in the lobstrosity version of the lobster's meral spread, clearly a challenge to fight. However, Roland quickly regains his moxie and crushes its back with a large rock. For good measure he stomps the head with his left foot, still shod in a whole boot. It emits buzzes of pain, King tells us, and barfs up some gobs of sand and pebbles from its serrated beak. Yuck. So much for that lobstrosity. It's toast, and deservedly so. *However, we're told it felt pain.* Could this be true?

"Who among you has read Mr. King? Raise a claw if you have. No one? Well, on we trudge through literal and cultural darkness. King is a terrific novelist. But what does he know about crustacean pain, if indeed a lobstrosity is even a crustacean? In truth, no more nor less than anyone else. Pain and also suffering, pain's consequent, are phantom events, emotional and therefore entirely mental. Roland's perceived pain at the locations of his missing digits was all in his head, the only place where pain actually can be manifested. His brain was simply reminding him where the damage occurred. Those bleeding sites felt nothing, the mangled nerves just messengers relaying the bad news to headquarters. This suggests that possessing the necessary brain function is prerequisite for experiencing pain, in which case the sensation has a neurological underpinning relying on specialized sensory neurons. These are called the 'primary nociceptors,' or simply the 'nociceptors.'"

Day Tripper interrupts: "Whoa, hang on un momento, Mister-Doctor-Professor-know-it-all. What in the fuck are these noci-what-the-fucks?"

"I just said, special nerve cells that detect tissue damage and presage pain. Think of them collectively as an early warning system of more serious damage. Feeling pain in the absence of nociceptors is apparently impossible. However, sensory neurons of all types require an appropriate wiring arrangement and a system for internally processing signals received from outside and relaying them upstairs. Among vertebrates that central receiver is the brain."

"Hold it there, Professor. It's me, Day Tripper. Like a good li'l lobster I raised my claw to ast a question and thought maybe youse had seen it. Anyhow, witout noci-thingies there can't be no pain?"

"No need to announce your identity. I recognize your voice. But that's right. Very astute." Sonny knows that complimenting Day Tripper annoys the Professor. After a brief silence, the Professor continues.

"In fact, there's a rare human condition known as congenital insensitivity to pain, or congenital analgesia, in which afflicted persons are born with nonfunctioning nociceptors. These individuals are likely to die young when unable to recognize and extricate themselves from lethal situations because their early warning system of pain presaging impending danger is inactive.

"But let's get back on track. Conceptually, the notion of pain can be partitioned into three stages. Stage one is simply detecting the painful stimulus. This is nociception, a purely reflexive, physical response. Nociceptors are advising the brain, 'Tell your boy, owner of this body, to depart the scene pronto because bad stuff is about to happen.' Stage two is the actual sensation of pain, which lags a split-second behind nociception. That's the brain saying, 'Oops, too late. Your boy is hurting some, but had he not moved immediately away from the stimulus — meaning the source of his pain — the damage would be lots worse. He could have been severely injured, even killed. Be grateful for nociception's warning.' Nociception followed by pain has obvious fitness value in evolutionary terms, allowing the recipient to survive and possibly reproduce, thus passing along its genes and helping to keep the species viable."

Day Tripper interjects: "Surviving *witout* passing

along my genes was my goal as a human. Now that I'm a lobster I don't give a rat's ass. I figure the world can't have too many lobster dinners, so I'm happy to do my part."

The Professor ignores him. "Stage three is suffering, the emotional consequent of pain. Suffering is the brain thinking, 'Damn this hurts, woe is me.' Like pain, stage three is a mental experience. However, an alternate form of suffering can arise even in the absence of those first two stages. Think of, 'I'm so sad because my lover has left me.' A state of suffering, surely, but not a manifestation of physical hurting in the way Roland suffered afterward from the pain of his trigger finger being chomped off."

Day Tripper says, "I'm always grateful when a homie bimbo departs my shelter. Good riddance. And that dude Roland, he's lucky it's his trigger finger got lopped off instead of his trigger. Ha! Nothing worse than a stubby gonophore. Did I say it right?"

"That's correct, his gonophore," says the Professor, a touch wearily.

Sonny breaks in and says, "What's an example of this pain sequence? The simpler the better."

"A classic case," says the Professor, "is the hot stove, although as lobsters it requires remembering what it was like to have fingers. I was deficient in this respect throughout most of my life. At one time, as a youth, I had all ten, then later just five."

Day Tripper turns to Sonny. "What's he talking about?"

The Professor says, "Never mind, just a little joke. Anyway, it goes like this. Revert for a moment to your human days. You accidentally touch a hot stovetop. The nociceptive response is instantaneous, and you jerk your hand away. The movement is entirely reflexive, involving no thought whatever. A split-second afterward you feel pain in your fingers. Not actually your fingers, of course, but in your brain, the signal having been delivered to the brain from the damaged nociceptors in your fingers. The meaning is clear: if you think this hurts, imagine how much worse your hand would feel if you hadn't removed it from the stove immediately. Now commences a period of lingering pain, which keeps you awake nights and disturbs your focus during the day. Your fingers are covered with analgesic cream and bandages. You can't use the hand during tasks normally taken for granted. Your life, having been interrupted, makes you despondent. Ergo, you *suffer* until the hand heals and everyday existence returns to normal.

"Considering our present circumstances, yours and mine, I believe it's appropriate to ask if we lobsters have a brain developed sufficiently to process pain and sustain suffering. The answer? Doubtfully, in my opinion, and that of many other scientists. Compared with the mammalian brain, a cohesive, layered, centrally organized signal processing depot, the lobster's equivalent of a 'brain' consists of fifteen decentralized nerve clusters, or ganglia, distributed throughout the body. . . ."

"Hold it! Hold on! Oy Prof, youse is telling us that lobsters got no fucking brains? That we're sorta thinking wit our asses, or what?"

"Pretty much, Day Tripper," the Professor says. "When we ask if a particular species of animal can suffer, we're not merely asking if it can *feel* pain, but also *if it's aware of the pain*. If unaware, then suffering, the subsequent stage, isn't possible. Can a lobster's separate clusters of ganglia adequately process pain and suffering? I don't believe so, although no one can say with certainty. However, the evidence indicates strongly that such sensations are very likely beyond animals lacking primary nociceptors. Their presence appears to be mandatory for pain to occur and, subsequently, suffering.

"Insects evolved from crustaceans, and insect and crustacean ganglion clusters are wired similarly. Insects possess nociceptors, but so far they haven't been found in any crustacean species, hinting that their putative existence in this group is entirely inferential. Let this fact sink in. But never say never until you're certain. An axiom of science says that absence of evidence isn't necessarily evidence of absence."

"Sorry to interrupt again, Prof, but I gotta get it straight. So, youse gotta have noci-thingies to feel pain, but we lobsters ain't got any. So, we can't feel pain, right?"

"That's the supposition: without nociception, no pain. Actual lobsters around here — the 'homies,' you call them — probably aren't aware of pain and therefore don't feel it. Without a brain a lobster can't be conscious, hence it can't suffer, also a mental experience."

"Yeah," says Day Tripper, "and on top of all that since becoming a lobster I got fucking *bugs* in my family tree? There was, like, this kid in grade school, Tommy McPhearson. He was little and hairy wit ears that stuck straight out like a taxi wit both doors open. He looked sorta like a monkey, so we — me and my homeboys — named him Monk, and it stuck. Everyone started calling the kid that, even the teachers. His fucking mom fucking hated us."

"Interesting, but back to the subject. If crustacean nociceptors prove conclusively not to exist then pain and suffering are highly unlikely. Presently, so-called 'evidence' of crustacean pain is derived after exposing test animals to noxious stimuli and observing behavior described as pain-like responses. Observations are then compared against known mammalian responses under similar conditions, a kind of gold standard for identifying pain. However, this method of reasoning, 'proof by analogy,' is a logical fallacy by assuming that because two objects or events are alike in some ways they're alike in others. Having been obtained indirectly, observational data offer no functional insight into proof of mechanism, such as invoking isolated primary nociceptors to fire as evidence of nociception. In other words, what stimulated the behavior, and consequently, what did the behavior actually signify? These things can't be known from observation alone.

"And what about insect nociceptors? Do they measure up? Are they even operational? Responses to putative painful situations often fail to induce the expected behavioral reactions. A female praying mantis devours her mate while *in flagrante delicto*, starting with his head. Seemingly nonplussed, her lover keeps pumping. Cockroaches consume their own internal organs after experiencing abdominal ruptures."

"Jesus fucking Mary and Joseph! And they're my relations?"

Sonny says, "Not to worry, dude, only distantly."

"Right," says the Professor. Suddenly distracted, he feels trapped in a psychological labyrinth of ignorance, a place dark and deep, coursing through tunnels of hollow silence. His lecture has the clear linearity of a story properly told: statement of purpose, definitions, a sequence in which A leads to B, B to C, then nuances, relevance, interpretation, and closing. And Day Tripper — a moron, a goddamn philistine — blows it up. This talking at cross purposes: what's the point of verbal communication, the richness of language, if neither communicant understands the other? What the hell am I doing here at the bottom of the ocean dressed in chitin?

"Where was I? Oh yes, honeybees purposely crippled by experimenters and offered honey laced with morphine were blasé about eating it despite possessing opiate receptors. Are these insects actually in pain? Not based on present knowledge. And what about suffering? Also unlikely. If nociception is indeed functioning, what are the biomarkers? Obviously, standard behavioral criteria based on observation are unreliable.

"Okay, so primary nociceptors have yet to be found in any species of crustacean, and current wisdom says that without them there can be no sensation of pain, much less suffering. But let's dig deeper. As mentioned, the belief that invertebrates feel pain is inferentially derived from behavioral responses and compared with those of species we believe confidently are capable of painful experiences, mainly humans and other mammals, and also birds. However, to repeat: such 'proof by analogy' is indirect and not empirically derived. We usually can tell if another human is in pain, but we can't experience it ourselves. We're capable of sympathy, certainly, but it ends there. Recall Nagel's conclusion about what's it's like to be a bat.

"What bat?" says Day Tripper. "How do we get from insects to bats? I'm lost, Prof." Then he says under his breath to Sonny, "The Prof is a bat hisself. A dingbat."

"Who said that?" says the Professor. "State your name and station at once!" He presents an invisible meral spread and pisses fiercely onto the decapodium.

"What'd I tell youse?" Day Tripper whispers to Sonny, who gives him a pseudo-knee in his pseudo-ribs.

The Professor recovers quickly and says, "Day Tripper, you remind me of the scarecrow in the Wizard of Oz who wished for a brain. But okay, about Nagel and bats. Thomas Nagel is an American philosopher who argued in a famous article that humans will never know what it feels like to be a bat, that only a bat can ever know, but even then not to the extent of experiencing another bat's pain or other emotions, assuming it has them. By extrapolation, no human can know what it's like being a lobster, and neither can another lobster when the issues are pain and suffering."

"Who was he arguing wit, this Nagel dude?" says Day Tripper.

There's a minor hydrodynamic disturbance from the decapodium as the Professor throws up his claws in frustration. After a moment he continues. "Even if it's someday shown that lobsters do have nociceptors, this doesn't guarantee they feel pain unless pain is defined using yet undiscovered criteria; otherwise, we're left with an early warning system that stops short of segueing into pain, such as the apparent situation with mantids, roaches, and honeybees. In a wider philosophical context, how would we know what lobsters experience? We understand pain and suffering to be subjective *and entirely personal*. Telling other individuals you feel their pain is disingenuous. Realistically, we can feel only our own."

Sonny says, "Yes, but what you and I think ought to count, right? We're reasoning creatures trapped in the bodies of a species that's deficient in important respects, namely intellect, consciousness, and the capacity to speak and transmit abstract thoughts and emotions."

"Yes," the Professor says, "what you say is true, except that our special status also hamstrings us as the ultimate confounding variable in this thought experiment. Exactly because we're still able to think like humans introduces bias into the interpretation of our sensory experiences as lobsters, tainting them. For example, reprise your phenomenological and emotional experiences of molting the first time."

"What do youse mean, 'reprise' it?" says Day Tripper.

"Go back to your first molt and tell us what you were feeling."

"Scared shitless. One of youse told me a lobster can suffocate and die if it gets stuck halfway outta its shell."

"I felt anxious before molting and relief afterward," Sonny says.

"All probably normal experiences for formerlies," the Professor says. "But was molting painful? Did you try to escape it by back-flipping away? Did you buzz in fearful agony? Importantly, during these times of enhanced concern for the welfare of animals, *did you feel pain and suffer as a result*?"

Sonny says, "I guess Day Tripper and I felt only fear, anxiety, and relief, but no pain. I felt some discomfort and frustration, like a human struggling to pull off very tight clothes, but I didn't hurt. Did you, Day Tripper?"

"Naw," Day Tripper says.

"It's not uncommon for discomfort to precede pain," says the Professor, "although it seems irrelevant in our situation as formerly human. Let's address a question that concerns any reasoning lobster of commercial legal size. What does it experience when boiled alive? Behaviorally, lobsters become agitated on being dropped into boiling water, activity that doesn't necessarily equate with pain and suffering. Lobsters in nature thermoregulate as a matter of course, often seeking more salubrious temperatures. While searching, their activity increases. You've undoubtedly noticed this yourselves. But the lobster in the hot-pot. . . .As the water boils does it feel pain associated with its calefaction, the congealing and hardening of its mucilaginous tissues, the denaturing of its proteins? The superficial answer would be, yes, of course it does! Certainly, how could it not?

"Reasoning through this morass, if we factor in what science can tell us about pain and factor out human emotion on the subject — which actually is irrelevant to the argument — the issue distills down to this: no brain, no pain; no pain, no pain-stimulated emotion. However, we'll doubtfully ever know. At the level of the individual, you'd have *to be* that specific lobster at that very instant it's plopped into the pot, and still you might not feel anything except an urge to seek cooler water. Remember, no organism can experience another's pain. Period. Too bad we can't ask the eponymous protagonist in Lecasble's novella *Lobster*, who escapes the pot after being only partly boiled. The author doesn't tell us what he felt, and as for Lobster himself, his mouthparts on the subject are sealed. I'll say this much: Day Tripper, you're a real pain, and I feel it right here in my telson. Class dismissed!"

18.

A BARNACLE HAS SETTLED on Sonny's carapace in the middle of the areola where he can't reach it. The Professor refuses to pluck it off, stating a need to be true to their lobsterly incarnation, including rules governing decapod behavior. One of these, he proclaims, prohibits mutual grooming by falsely bestowing tendencies of sympathy and altruism, obscuring the lobster's true cantankerous and selfish nature. Sonny has tried scraping it off against a rock, but without success. He has no choice except to carry this annoying tumescence until his next molt, which is months away.

It's late autumn. The previous winter had taught Sonny a lesson, and he refuses to spend another in shallow water. He abandons his current shelter at five fathoms and starts walking eastward toward the center of the Gulf and deeper water. As the days and nights pass he feels the barnacle growing and senses the relentless vibrations generated by its feathery feet as they extend and retract to capture and retrieve plankton. The effect is like living under elevated train tracks in a neighborhood where the trains never stop running.

In lobster society there are movers and dispersers. The former travel, but usually don't wander very far outside the home range; the latter often travel quite a distance, even hundreds of miles. The Professor is a mover, a homebody who changes residencies frequently but keeps within the same general vicinity. Early in his lifetime as a lobster he considered dispersing, on one occasion going north to the entrance of the Bay of Fundy, on another south to Mount Desert Island. At still another time he set out eastward intending to trek all the way to the Atlantic, but a close call with a trawl net before making it even halfway sent him scurrying back west. These days he moves around a bit, although seldom more than a couple of miles from Suramoh Island, venturing outside this radius only when seeking deeper, warmer water in winter.

The Professor's pattern is to pick a shelter he likes, stay a few days or weeks, then drift on when bored with the surroundings and choices of foods. Dining options are important. In his former human life he was a great admirer of food, not to the extent of snobbery, nor did he ever consider himself a gourmand, but he always ate well. These days he prefers carryout, so while shopping for a new shelter he also evaluates the neighborhood's grocery situation, the availability and variety of its offerings. Once settled he hunts-and-gathers maybe twice a week, collecting enough crabs, mussels, clams, polychaetes, or whatever suits his fancy to last a while. If he's near shallow water he might snip off a sprig of rockweed or sea lettuce with his cutter claw for garnish. You can identify his current lodgings by the shambolic midden outside the entrance. He takes some comfort in knowing that humans are nearby, here beside the land's stony interface where settlers once struggled ashore through sticky gray fog, shouting prosodic hymns of strife and misery.

Sonny, in contrast, is more a disperser. He likes

traveling and experiencing new places. With winter on the way, he's feeling the urge. Downeast Maine is a place of snaggle-toothed inlets, broad bays, and stepping-stone islands, one of which is Suramoh Island. The sea's bedrock is granite, and some of the islands are isolated granite plutons. On the way east Sonny scrabbles over agglomerations of rubble that slope ever downward, expanses of stones and boulders interspersed with depressions of sand and overlying silt, reminders of long-ago glaciers that retreated landward as they melted, dropping their loads of rocks and boulders to form these plains of till and glacial drift. They will thin as he proceeds, then reappear, remnants of those stony underbellies of glaciers that fractured into icebergs, melting as they floated seaward.

His surroundings gradually darken as he descends, and by seventeen fathoms the kelp and other seaweeds have disappeared, unable to photosynthesize in the constant dimness. An exception is sea colander kelp, or shotgun kelp, named for the remarkable fenestration of its fronds. Isolated individuals can still be found at twenty-two fathoms. At this depth the light absorbed and the light reflected cancel each other's effect; objects appear to tumble downward until meeting and swallowing their shadows. Sonny needs to be wary as the seascape deepens. Fish predation on lobsters intensifies in deep offshore waters where large fishes are more abundant than they are inshore, the Professor's poo-pooing of the danger notwithstanding. He continues to amble nervously down the cobbled slope aware of his increased vulnerability when in the open, zigzagging into bouldered regions, the better to duck quickly into a convenient cave or crevice.

Still, persistent signals other than visual are unmistakable: a swirling eddy that tickles his mechanoreceptors, a whiff of mucus sloughed naturally by swimming fishes and detected by chemoreceptors in his antennules. These trigger his alarm system instantaneously, leaving split seconds to react. Then fear intercedes between stimulus and response, vaporizing shock and crystalizing the next moment into irreversible action. This time, contact: a cod's chin barbel brushes his second antennae as he flips backward into a crevice. My god, it tasted him! Never before has he considered himself a morsel, an object to be crushed between jaws, swallowed, reduced to a state of fatal disassembly, dissolved and digested and finally dispensed into the currents as unrecognizable residue.

Life is a scrabble for potential energy. The tiniest are consumed and adsorbed by the next largest stepwise up the food chain. Every living entity is a nervous package of calories draped in futile disguises. Hope? Unknown. The next higher step in the ladder will detect you and reach down. It's true: he really is a passel of matter like everything else, a composite of universally available molecules sorted by functional necessity then pressed together and shaped into the physical mass recognizable as him. Nothing extraordinary. How disgusting. How unfair. Surely, there exist entities similar to him, special ones destined to live above the fray. But no, every living thing down here is mindless and indifferent, tissue pressed from a common template collated into infinite shapes and sizes and unique only in their species-specific phenotypes. His life, like any other, is trivial and fleeting. Is being a dominant lobster really a big deal? He suddenly feels small, as he had after that first molt. The surfaces of the crevice into which he's wedged is alive with sessile organisms. He brushes against a colony of sea anemones, and those closest retract in an act of self-preservation, as if their lives somehow matter.

Sonny is depressed and has a case of the sorries. He's feeling low, sunken clear to bedrock. He's suffering a bout of anemoia. Although accepting the totality of his lobsterhood and its consequences, he regrets that he never had a real human girlfriend, one with only two arms and two legs. He mourns that first beer never drunk, the first cigar forever unsmoked, the moustache never to be nurtured. Of the small cache of memories retained, he misses clouds and snowflakes and scratching his balls.

Out of boredom he decides to ignore his sensory systems, pretend they've been disabled, except that lacking eyelids his eyes will still be open. Pay no attention to the rest of the flashing dashboard lights, he tells himself, and promptly stubs the dactyl of his third walking leg, the left one probably, or could have been the right. It didn't hurt, but nonetheless he considers the event worth weeping over, if only he could, poor him. That's rich because nothing's funnier than a crustacean crying crocodilian tears and limping falsely as a plaintive mother killdeer all the while berating the indifferent sea's inanition, not to mention its major deficiencies in the humor and sympathy departments. No matter. He doesn't feel like laughing anyway. The experiment fails; the dashboard lights blink on. Dusk is gulping down the remaining visible objects one by one as the tenebrous night corkscrews toward him to lap up the leftovers.

Sonny moves on, senses on high alert in this strange world, occasionally encountering other lobsters. Not wishing to interact, each turns its telson to the other without even an antennal touch and proceeds on its way. The only sounds so far have been the usual background noises: continuous clicking of shrimps, low-frequency grunts and groans of fishes, stones settling into pockets of bedrock to await eternity. However, on an otherwise unremarkable night he wanders into a zone of exceptional vibrations. Like the other sounds these too are low-frequency but seems to be a composite of numerous sources, as you might expect from a school of fish. Oddly, it has the characteristic frequency and amplitude of lobsters buzzing. However, a group of lobsters is unlikely. Lobsters are asocial. He has sensed the disturbance for several days and nights. The rapid propagation of sound underwater has hindered his ability to pinpoint the direction and distance, but now he seems closer to the nexus. The vibrations are emanating from a hill of boulders straight ahead.

Mechanosensors tingling, he strides through a high vertical crevice, which after a short distance opens into a large enclosed space with a sandy floor. The vibrations abruptly cease. Sonny realizes that he's blundered into a cave crowded with lobsters. What he sensed is the sum of their combined buzzing, although he's now starting to pick up elements of disjointed conversations. This is a gathering of formerlies! He had considered if formerlies might form group friendships and discussed the possibility with the Professor, arguing that humans are social and somewhere lobster formerlies might be getting together to alleviate loneliness. The Professor vehemently disagreed, claiming that asocial behavior is the norm once you become a lobster. Social interaction? Lobsters? Impossible! Nonetheless, here he is surrounded by conspecifics in a clearly nonconfrontational atmosphere, and he has instantly become the object of their attention. He involuntarily emits a buzz, hoping immediately it hasn't made him seem cowardly. He undoubtedly is the biggest, baddest lobster present, but that is slight assurance if suddenly the mob decides to attack and eat him.

Then a voice says, "Welcome, friend. Some of us have been picking up vibrations of your presence in the distance."

Sonny is flabbergasted. "Who are you?"

"Just a bunch of formerlies having a get-together."

Says Sonny, "I didn't know lobsters ever got together, formerlies or homies."

"Homies?" his interlocuter says.

"You know, regular lobsters," Sonny says.

"Ha! That's good!" the other snorts appreciatively, and Sonny detects similar vibrations all around. Is it lobster laughter? For the first time since transitioning he feels a sense of comity putatively impossible for his species. He apparently has stumbled into some sort of crustacean locutory, as in a monastery or church, where social interaction is encouraged instead of forbidden, and no one is punished for it. Or maybe it's an offbeat conventicle of some sort where formerlies can meet and hide from their enemies. But what enemies?

"My name's Joshua. The rest — roughly two dozen who gather periodically here in my shelter — will introduce themselves shortly. It's potluck. Everyone brings food to share, but that won't be required of you, not the first time, and especially considering you didn't know of our existence."

"You share food?" Sonny says. Then adds, "Instead of fighting over it?"

"Yes. And thoughts. Thoughts and stories. We get lonely for our former lives, and these gatherings make us feel better. Don't you ever get lonely? Oh, I told you my name and forgot to ask yours. How rude." He has begun a haptic examination of Sonny, touching him lightly with his antennae, still without urinating in his direction as would be expected of a male lobster whose shelter has just been invaded. Sonny is finding this experience confusing and disquieting. And vaguely unpleasant. He gives Joshua's face a blast of piss. Joshua backs away, emitting a surprised buzz. The room is suddenly buzzing, yet no one else has urinated.

Sonny realizes that although his behavior is perfectly normal and even expected in these circumstances, he's committed a *faux pas*. But how to rectify it? Apologize? Certainly not! It would be unlobsterly. After all, it's Joshua who has encroached on his personal space despite the shelter technically being his. No one else has stepped forward to claim it and challenge for its defense. Maybe it's actually community owned. How strange that would be. Throughout their conversation Sonny has maintained a suitable social distance and made no threatening gestures until now. Best to deflect and decompress the mounting hostility by simply answering Joshua's question. He considers he can do this without relinquishing his self-perceived status as a dominant lobster. The others are surely aware of his considerably larger size, and he's given them one shot across the bow by pissing in the face of their leader.

"My name is Sonny, and no, I don't get lonely. I very much enjoy being by myself without the responsibility of friends. I never have a need to ask after another formerly's feelings, health, and well-being. Screw that. I'd as soon not deal with those things. I only know two other formerlies, both casual acquaintances. They're loners too, same as the homies, and we never make plans to meet. In fact, these guys intensely dislike each other. When I bump into either it's entirely accidental. We

usually say a couple of howdies before splitting in opposite directions like proper lobsters. So, what's with this
hoe-down and the touchy-feely stuff? I'm not used to it."

"But you could be!" says Joshua. "You don't always
have to behave like a curmudgeon. You could join the
group and reconstitute some of your human qualities by
joining in our rituals."

"Such as?"

"Group hugs. Forming a circle and holding claws.
Community buzzing. That sort of thing."

Sonny shudders. Wait until the Professor hears
about this, he thinks. "Thank you for the invitation," he
says, "but I'll pass."

He moves deeper over the next few nights, foraging
as he goes and ever alert for signals that a big cod could
be in the area. He has been spending more time in rocky
habitats, both for their superior choice of prey and sur-
feit of safe shelter spaces. Lobsters are less plentiful than
in the shallows where numbers can reach one individual
per square yard. When coming to open places on the
seafloor he continues quickening his pace, often crossing
them without stopping, hurrying to the next outcrop or
cluster of boulders.

He comes across an old anchor festering with
pustules of spalling rust. Blessed be oxidation and the
unsuspecting ignorance of iron. Up he goes, climbing an
arm for the helluva it, launching himself from the bill,
floating, landing in a soft wallow of finger sponges. He's
in a rhythm, feeling the sea's ineffable ululations drum-
ming against his mechanosensors, aware that beneath
him lies the righteous warp of its ancient geology stretching and contracting, the buckling upward and subsidence
of bedrock in a time when time was the only thing and

no one knew what to call it because no one was here. He trudges across the basins of rifts, sinking into fluffy sediment. It roils in intermittent pulses against his che-mosensors, exhaling redolent gasps of birth and decay. He scrabbles over unyielding fields of cobbles, trans-verses razed mansions of boulders, scales mountains. All around and sloshing inside him is the sea's wash and reverence. He smells and tastes its mineral subtlety, is buffeted in eddies of playful currents by whirligig gen-tility, stands statocyst-balanced on the metaphysics of a seesaw's fulcrum where life and death tip in opposing directions at the whim of an unseeable *quimboiseur* who comes seeping, creeping, peeping.

In fisherfolk lingo, most of the lobsters he's encoun-tering are chix, quarters, or halves. Some are bigger — selects and jumbos, a few nearly his own size of fif-teen pounds. He also notices that the water is indeed warmer than it is inshore, probably fifty degrees Fahr-enheit, or thereabouts, as the Professor had predicted. Excellent! No more days and nights of half-frozen torpor, no battering from winter storms. He goes deeper over the next couple of nights, passing through the thermo-cline at around fifty fathoms and feeling the temperature plummet. Too cold to search for housing, so he retreats back up the slope.

One night he happens on a high ridge of serried boulders surrounded and interspersed by sharply slop-ing screes. He climbs to its top at fourteen fathoms and finds it riddled with crevices that on cursory inspection appear to be tight, black, and depthless, as if designed by a wizened architect of decapod housing. Moreover, food is plentiful everywhere, a smorgasbord of tasty crusta-ceans, mollusks, and other creatures.

He decides to stay until spring; that is, he and the barnacle, his unwelcome traveling companion. Come spring and warmer temperatures, he will definitely move back inshore and molt.

Meanwhile, dreams arrive in waves disturbing him while awake and asleep until he no longer knows his immediate status, or if they aren't dreams at all but a form of distressing reality. His lobsterly heart seems to thrum from a sequestered place outside himself: ta-da-dum it beats, ta-da-dum. Yes, controlled by witchy fingers and unshelved thoughts. Ta-da-dum. There needs to be a new poetics, one invented just for spineless interlopers, the diaspora of those having outside-in skeletons. Engendering free verse, those swathed in chitin will lecture the bony endoskeleters on the ontology of punctuated evolution.

And so it comes to pass that a damper is necessary, a metaphorical lid or sorts. His emotions feel recently soldered together and still hot. He imagines smelling and tasting vaporizing lead, and it sends him reeling, tottering, falling over dizzy, flapping like a hooked fish or else compressed and flattened, stuck in place like roadkill fused to macadam. Angry, gnarly, weak altogether, no self-confidence either. He's servile, contemptible; a distracted, discombobulated, dysfunctional decapod who never smoked but now wonders where he might obtain a cigarette, put some spring in his schtick, cool-like, dangling James Deanly from a third maxilliped of his mouthparts.

He approaches a whelk and notices that it's a waved whelk, a common species in the Gulf of Maine. Hey buddy, got a cig? And a light? He waves his cutter claw, but the waved whelk doesn't wave back, could be from lack of appendages for waving. Rude behavior, nonetheless. Might at least have wiggled its eyestalks in acknowledgment, but ignores him as if he's flotsam and continues sliding along on its slimy muscular foot. It's big and ugly, but still just a snail. Maybe he ought to just eat the damn thing and forget dreaming about a cigarette. Healthier that way, although what could be the harm in tobacco if you don't have sensitive oral mucosa, salivary glands, a throat, and lungs to defile?

The whelk seems to have sped up. It's really humping, a cheetah among mollusks, maxed out at a yard an hour, destined to be out of sight sooner than later. Decision time, easy enough. Everything in lobsterworld is treated as food unless up-close-look-listen-taste-smell-feel proves otherwise. He grabs the whelk in his crusher claw. CRUNCH! Taste receptors in the first two pairs of walking legs trigger a clasping response in the tiny pinchers, stimulating them to eagerly probe the substrate. They push aside scraps of shell, scrabbling for the pieces of pulverized flesh now wafting amino acids upward and into his face. The pincers close on them, direct them to his mouthparts. With nervous energy the pincers open and close, hop and skip, twitch, advance and retreat in a mindless, rapacious dance. They pick up a tidbit, drop it, pick it up again and move it to the mouthparts where chemosensory setae accept it as suitable for shoving between the mandibles; alternatively, the mouthparts reject and discard the offering. Undeterred, the tiny pincers grab it again, drop it, pick it up, turn it over, taste-test with their setae before grasping and shoving it into the mouthparts for another assessment.

He tells himself he has nothing to do with these frantic, implacable activities, although he wonders: who — or what — is making these decisions. Not under his control, for sure, and not his fault that his ganglia-for-brains are insular instead of an integrated continent. Primitive wiring must be at fault. The macerated whelk leaks swirling tendrils of blood; guts and sliced flesh spill onto the seafloor looking like sections of petals torn from a pale flower, the juxtaposition incomprehensible. In a flash he understands his dilemma: living as an omnivore-scavenger is tough when you aspire to be a basically nice person. Seems odd, but can a lobster get sick to any of its three stomachs? No, has proclaimed the Professor. Forge ahead foraging and don't look behind you even if that were possible.

He's visited in his shelter by a premolt female, whose presence is out of season. Maybe she's a phantom, a dream image. "Hum sweetly against my carapace," she buzzes. "Either side, right or left. Yes, that's the place, right below the eye. Let the vibrations ricochet against the statocyst underneath. Your buzzing will stimulate the setae inside it and set those microscopic, acceleration-sensitive statoliths in motion. That'll upset my balance a little, make me dizzy, give me a rush. Ah, it tingles! Oh goodness! I remember when a human boyfriend would blow in my ear and give me the shivers. Sort of like you're doing now."

He's horny and hornswoggled; bedraggled, benighted, bewildered. Or thinks he is. Hell, let's just say he's confused. Could he be suffering from decapod dissociative disorder? Just his luck for a ganglion to misfire, possibly necessitating telepathic talk therapy. Goddammit. His dreams rankle and flabbergast him, misplace and shuffle him. Sometimes he feels human and thinks he sees other humans untransitioned and not dead but living right here, under the sea. However, he realizes that what he sees are illusions. As he considers this he shivers imperceptibly. In war, each day encompasses eternity and also the final nanosecond of life. Why is he thinking about war? He's had no experience of it, has never until now given it a thought. Is he getting religious, becoming a born-again lobster? What comes next? Rolling down the aisle of a chapel somewhere under this liquid horizon, tugging at his rostrum, flailing, gibbering in tongues? *In tongues*, that's a good one! If only. . . .

In a dream the kelp rises tall and patulous, marinating in slimy greenness as it surges upward toward the light, gas floats shuddering in the strictures of their buoyancy equations. Alginate on the hoof (rather, the holdfast), fronds sucking up the scarce photons like soda through a straw with nary a slurp, snort, or snuzzle. Some of the stipes part as if on cue framing a woman's face, a lovely human woman whose black mane surges back and forth in synchrony with the sea's monotonous motion. She's a congerish cougar; that is, there's a conger eel entwined serpent-like around her neck. It grins toothily. She's wearing a t-shirt that says HI, I'M PROTO-EVE! Otherwise, she's Garden-of-Eden-pre-Fall-from-Grace-bare-ass-naked. Evidently, he's been returned to a time before God sent His landscapers to weed out wickedness by uprooting the thickets where people fucked. These green-thumbed stormtroopers nearly succeeded, but they forgot the kelp forests. The Garden must have been inland.

She winks and blows a kiss, showering him in a cascade of silvery scales that flip and skid, stuttering the light like phosphenes. The effect on his proprioceptors is stroboscopic disco, making him disoriented and dizzy. He feels as if he's falling slowly from a great height, twisting and tumbling, now upside-down, now rightside-up. He thinks he might puke a little in his mandibles, inside his dream.

Suddenly, equilibrium: the statocysts in his cheeks have regained control and pulled back the joystick. He sighs a suspiration (redundancy be damned), which considering his present physical state can only happen at dreamtimes. He looks around and sees she's still there. She flashes a thigh provocative as a neon beer sign. Then, as she turns slightly away, he watches in fascination as she lifts that alterity of a leg (it might have been a fin in disguise) and farts. Bubbles of methane trickle upward — real natural gas — expanding as the impinging pressure diminishes, becoming lost in unbearable brightness. Without eyelids he's blinded, the ommatidia in his compound eyes gyrating when directed toward the sun. He quickly shifts his gaze downward to the kelp forest, seeking her, seeing only an afterimage. Despite trying mightily, he is unable to slip fully into this alternate reality, to perceive it through a disheveled consciousness. Perhaps there are no magic animals if the magical capacity to become them has been lost.

19.

HE'S BACK IN THE vicinity of Suramoh Island and wanders out of the shelter to forage. Although pleasantly warm, the seawater in this place seems thick and stagnant as if life has shut its doors and gone away. It tastes of hydrocarbons and decay and exudes a whiff of annealed magma. A gluey light edges sideways through the kelp canopy overhead, dripping morosely off the fronds and shinnying down the stipes before fading to monochromatic boredom. In the near visual field plumose sea anemones resembling pink and white powder puffs ripple in the current. Outside his frontal carapace someone is yelling, "Okay, put 'em up!" This wannabe adversary strides forward deploying the meral spread and expecting abjection, but Sonny is having none of it. They turn to face each other, the Professor's chitinous countenance a web of fine spidery lines like the crazing in old porcelain. He really could use a new shell.

"Put 'em down, professor," Sonny says laconically. "it's me, Sonny."

"Sonny? I once knew a lad named Sonny." The Professor lowers his claws and assumes his affected thinking pose, placing the dactyl of a walking leg against the forward part of his carapace. "Or was he a lobster?"

he says. "I hate it that lobster memory degrades completely after a week."

Sonny says, "That's homie lobsters, Professor, and it refers to agonistic interactions. We formerlies don't really have that excuse unless we get senile."

Nonetheless, the Professor raises his claws and charges forward uncertainly, a visually-impaired, decapodal Don Quixote. He stops and attempts to focus by wiggling his eyestalks, the lobster equivalent of blinking, then gives Sonny a pat-down with his antennae. "Don't try and fool me," he says. "I'll kick your telson so far up your cephalothorax you'll have to molt to find it again. To quote *Erec and Enide*, 'Tell me your station and your name, and I in turn will tell you mine!'"

An aged lobster unaware of their presence bumbles into view muttering, "Bless my soul, bless my soul." His antennae brush against them. Suddenly aware of others he draws back, turns hesitantly, and lumbers off in another direction, abdomen bouncing off the substrate. The professor shouts into the gloaming after him, "You have no soul; you're an invertebrate!" He then turns to Sonny: "A former, of course, origin unknown. Senile, no doubt."

"Don't be so crabby," Sonny says.

"I have reason to be. You wouldn't understand. As a youth I was plagued by the scrofula, always suppurating pus. I hid my condition by wearing baggy clothes. That's in addition to missing some serious appendages, as I've already told you. . .I think. On becoming a university professor I lurched through the halls on a crutch, bumping into walls while trying to avoid the blithe idiots bumping into me. Jesus, my life was awful, but the students were oblivious to anyone's debilities. Know what I really miss, which is impossible to find down here? A marvelous dinner followed by a slow-smoking cigar with a steady draw and a snifter of dark rum. I've probably said this before. Who can remember?"

Sonny picks a recently settled barnacle from his carapace and pops it into his mouthparts. "I get that, I suppose. Down here lots of what we eat is scavenged."

"Scavenged? Hell, think a minute: most of what 'civilized' humans eat is scavenged too, just more hygienic because they don't eat it directly off the ground. Humans gather or slaughter something then change its form and even composition into something else barely recognizable by chopping it to pieces, cooking it, and adding spices and condiments. In terms of relative nourishment they might as well eat roadkill directly from the highway. No need to even pound it; the meat's already been tenderized by eighteen-wheelers. And it isn't just coincidence that whatever you've eaten in the past as a human, greasy from a paper bag or expensive and beautifully presented on exquisite china, all ends up as shit, regardless."

Sonny tells the Professor that he isn't the only dissatisfied lobster in these parts — which incidentally seem less salutary than he remembers. At least the Professor had attained rank and acclaim in the academic world while he, Sonny, never even had a girlfriend or tasted beer. At least the Professor had enjoyed the conflicting thrill and shame of sleeping comfortably on a soft mattress, cashing steady paychecks, and could point to some success in the accumulation of goods and services despite having relinquished them after transitioning.

The Professor listens absently. He rubs a walking leg back and forth along his rostrum as if summing the totality of paradise on an abacus. He speaks: "Laddy, some of what you define as my successes are true, meager through they were. In sum, however, my life has been a saga of missed glory and sharp disappointments. Admittedly, I once was atop my profession, the very pinnacle, a renowned aphorist and Professor of Aphorismology, a shining light of Downeast University's faculty with appointments in both the humanities and the sciences. Unfortunately, as a science my specialty encountered headwinds when its hypotheses, stated in aphoristic format, yielded results that often weren't reproducible. The equilibrium equations of chemistry are reversible, and this has served that science handsomely. Sadly, the same can't be said about aphoristics. Take, for example, the classic 'it is better to have loved and lost than never to have loved at all,' which is easily turned on its head: 'it is better never to have loved at all than to have loved and lost.' Obviously, not much rigor."

The Professor emphasizes that he certainly doesn't miss academic politics, his revolting former chair in the humanities included. Luckily, he had remained a faculty member long enough to experience this adversary's demise, an obnoxious charlatan who chortled that he would outlive them all, a shabby mannequin dusted with dandruff. He kept the nails of his pinkies long for digging out earwax during faculty meetings, and his laugh would embarrass a hyena. Each day he wore the same raggedy suit that fit him like a circus tent fits an elephant. But death came sneaking, sniffing, nibbling at this sallow sack of fusing joints and spavined teeth.

Then one morning while seated in his office chair he suddenly tightened his butt cheeks, curled his toes, lashed his eyelids, and spazzed out. Heart went tachycardia into overdrive; it down-shifted and stalled on the grade, coughed, sputtered, blew its valves, and its pistons waved sayonara on a final upstroke. His secretary in the adjacent office reported his last words were muffled and faint but something like, chuck. . .you (hiccup). . .farley. Then a thump as he toppled onto his fake oriental rug laid atop the fake parquet floor, a fake nonsmile on his cold pale lips. His widow was called to the scene and gave the corpse a couple of kicks to the ribs.

His colleagues could only speculate as to any final thoughts. He had long held the position of Professor of Platitudes and was currently investigating why halts end with a screech, havoc is wreaked, and eschatology still matters if death is regularly unexpected. Most mysterious of all, why guesses should be hazardous, this last having considerable public safety implications. His final task appeared to be administrative. Spread out on the desk were a dozen or so applications for an empty faculty position, Assistant Professor of Redundant Tautologies.

"Those death throes were his one instant of glory," the Professor mused. "The coroner determined that he died of a transient refulgence."

20.

SONNY HAS BEEN MISSING his family. He realizes that visiting Mutha is out of the question. The logistics are impossible. Lobsters have excellent navigational skills. He could find her little dock easily, but leaving the water and climbing the hill to the chicken farm presents irremediable problems, such as breathing air and walking on land. Better to visit Uncle instead and ask if he knows how Mutha is faring. He has been reprising Uncle's penultimate statement that day he toppled over the side of *Sucatsa* and transitioned, what Uncle had said before advising him to backflip to the bottom and do it quickly. Uncle's words were cryptic and probably not to be taken literally. He said, "I'll leave a light on fah ye!" A light? What could that mean? No doubt a sign or signal of some kind. Uncle often spoke in a meandering, circumlocutory manner, conversations seldom following a logical trajectory. His orders often confused even Homer, his sternman, who had known Uncle all his life. After Uncle has muttered something incomprehensible and taken way too long to mutter it, Homer might say, "I cahnt figgah what ye're sayin, Uncle." Then Uncle might reply, "Well then, fah chrissakes, don't do as I say, do as I mean."

Sonny treks across the seafloor to Suramoh Island

and begins searching the offshore area for Uncle's traps, in particular any trap with the "light" or whatever the signal happens to be that Uncle mentioned immediately after he, Sonny, fell overboard. Most lobster traps look similar, and searching for the right one consumes all of several nights followed by several more. Eventually, he encounters a trap with a crude homemade sign attached to the top slats. Painted on it are some words nearly obscured by marine overgrowths. In the faint dawn they read: WELCUM HOM SUNNIE!

Sonny has molted during the summers of several successive years, growing substantially after each, and he probably weighs a solid twenty-five pounds including the massive claws. He's truly a sight in that transmigration of golden Trojan glory. As he approaches the trap, chemoreceptors in his antennules report that it still contains bait, and that the bait is reasonably fresh, indicating it isn't a "ghost" trap lost or abandoned. This information means that Uncle and Homer will eventually come to pick it up. Not being a swimmer, he knows he can't paddle to the surface and hang there treading water until *Sucatsa* happens along in the next day or two. Not having a reasonable alternative, he's letting himself purposely be trapped to gain a ride to the surface for a confab with Uncle and Homer, hear what news there is to hear, then it's back overboard and life as usual, which, the Professor reminds him often enough, differs little from life on land as a human; that is, eating, shitting, sleeping, fucking, and fighting.

He approaches the trap, stretches out his first pair of legs with claws closed and touching, and tries to squeeze inside, but the opening to the "tunnel" is a tetch small. He backs up and lunges at it while scrabbling his walking legs against the substrate until finally popping through. The place has a frantic, claustrophobic odor of imprisonment. Inside are three other inmates, all chix-size and male. On Sonny's arrival they panic, abandoning the bait secured in the trap's "kitchen" and retreating to the "parlor" section. There, despite mutual dislike, they huddle together in terror. Sonny ignores them and settles down in the "kitchen" to wait, meanwhile watching the dynamics of a trap nearby, where his presence as a dominant isn't affecting the behavior of lobsters approaching it from outside.

They come and go, entering and leaving with ease. The design of lobster traps assumes that once inside a lobster is too stupid to find its way out, but this is far from true. These devices are more revolving doors than traps. Underwater cameras have shown that only eleven percent of lobsters seen around commercial traps even enter them. Of these, two percent are captured. Maybe lobster traps are fairer devices than many people believe. Nonetheless, effort still matters: eighty percent of lobsters brought to land are caught by twenty percent of those fishing them. He who dies with the most toys has won the game is a saying that in general circumstances might or might not be valid. However, it seems true in lobster fishing because the devices are so inefficient. Consequently, the boat with the most traps baited and "soaking" below is likely to catch the most lobsters.

The sun is higher, the sea brighter when his mechanosensors detect a boat approaching, and he recognizes by the vibratory pattern of the engine that it's *Sucatsa*. The buoy line soon goes taut, and the trap ascends rapidly. When it breaks the surface Sonny gets a blurry glimpse of a man's face, but in the blinding morning light can't be certain whose. The winch raises the trap slightly higher than the gunnel, and deformed hands haul it aboard. "Holy shit!" It's not the sternman holding onto the trap who shouts this, but the man at the wheel, and he isn't Uncle. "Lookit that sonofabitch, Homah! That's the big-un we wanted, and he's a golden one to boot! Hot damn! Jackpot, baby! Good times comin'! I'm a'puttin' the hammah down and headin' fah home. Git him 'im out'n the pot and hold tight." He jams the throttle then sticks two fingers in his mouth and whistles shrilly.

"Homer, it's me, Sonny."

"I know," Homer says. "I gotta whispah so's the othah guy don't think I'm looney, talkin' to a lobstah." He looks around furtively, turning his almost-head and the rest of his body in unison.

"Where's Uncle?"

"He's down to the hospital in Baston. The doctahs is try'na figgah how to give 'im seven knee replacements. Uncle's condition has 'em stumped, if'n you get me meanin'."

"Funny, Homer. Very funny. Who's the other guy, and what's he doing here?"

"That's Abnah. He's a friend o' Uncle's, and his li'l gal is a'gittin' hitched next week. He's bin a'hopin' to catch a giant lobstah to be the centahpiece at the reception dinnah. He's all excited 'cause he now figgahs that'll be ye'self."

"Jesus Christ, Homer! We're kin! When you open the trap make like I slip out of your hands and fall over the side. I don't want to be a centerpiece at someone's goddamn banquet."

"Ye're buzzin' awful loud, Sonny. Calm down. I cahnt do that. He's Uncle's best friend, and he's been a'pullin' Uncle's pots, these ones, fah days to hep out, then he goes and pulls his own ones."

"Do you realize you're partaking in a potential

murder? I'm not exactly an ordinary lobster."

"Evah'one else'll think ye are. What kin I do?"

"I already told you. Pretend to fumble me then drop me over the side. The boat's bouncing around enough to make it seem an honest mistake. For chrissakes, *do it!*"

Instead, Homer lifts Sonny out of the trap and plops him into the livewell.

"You bastard!" Sonny says.

Abner can't help himself. Several times on the way to the dock he leaves the wheel to step back and peer into the livewell, and each time he shakes his head, laughs, and whistles. He gets his wife on the radio and tells her the good news. He instructs her and Niesha, his daughter, to meet him at the dock and gives them an ETA.

Sonny is feeling doomed. To be boiled alive for the amusement of a wedding party might be the most ignominious end possible for a lobster, especially a formerly who should know not to enter a trap. Hell, even most of the homies seem to understand that. Soon he will be gawked at by everyone loafing around the lobster pound as the boats come in to register and unload the day's catches. He, of course, will not be among those others dumped unceremoniously into the pound and held until loaded into refrigerated trucks and driven to market. No, he's special at least in this respect. Homer has suggested to Abner that they put Sonny in the aquarium on the dock where his lobster alter-ego had once resided and whose incarnation Sonny has become after staring too long through the glass. Another spin on memory's merry-go-round.

It's late afternoon, and a crowd has gathered around the aquarium. He hears the oohs and aahs and the expected snide remarks about how he might taste when cooked. Then Abner and his wife and daughter push through to the front. With his poor vision Sonny can discern only their smudged images, but he can detect their voices.

"He's a wicked pissah, deeah!" Abner's wife says. "What an amazin' coincidence. Jist last night we talked aboot catchin' a pehfect lobstah fah Niesha's reception, and heah ye went and done it."

"Yeah, he's pehfect alright," Abner says. "O'course me and Homah caught 'im in Uncle's trap usin' Uncle's boat, so to be honest he's Uncle's lobstah. I still got to phone down to that hospital in Baston and ast Uncle if'n we kin have 'im." He adds, "This one lobstah, I'm meanin'. He's a breedah, fah shooah, and legally we cahnt keep 'im, but I'm ready to pay the fine."

"Fah shooah," says his wife.

"Ye won't hafta." It's Niesha piping up. "I don't want a lobstah this big and this pretty to be a centah-piece at me weddin' reception. He should to be livin' out in the ocean. Daddy, thanks fah thinkin' o' me, but I want ye to let 'im go, and do it *now*. Just drap 'im off'n the dock. He'll fah shooah find his own way to deep watah. At his size he might be king o' all the lobstahs." With that, she turns and threads through the crowd and walks rapidly away down the dock, arms folded tightly against her chest.

"Well, I'll be damn," Abner says. "That's gratitude fah ye, but it's Niesha's day that's a'comin', and if that's what this li'l gal o' our'n wants, so be it. But I'm still a'phonin' Uncle down to Baston and tellin' 'im the news."

Homer, who is standing beside him, says, "Kin I talk to Uncle private-like when ye phone 'im?"

"Shooah. Come on home with us, and we'll do 'er now."

They reach Uncle in his hospital room. Abner gives him a rundown of the day's events, wrapping up by saying that Niesha wants the golden lobster released immediately, and he's prepared to honor her wish. And anyway, it isn't a legal keeper. He then passes the phone to Homer, and the family leaves the room to give him privacy.

Uncle asks if the lobster might be Sonny, and Homer answers in the affirmative. Uncle asks why Sonny wasn't released at sea immediately, and Homer tells him he was afraid to do it because Abner got so excited. Uncle then says to Homer that he's goddamn fortunate Sonny's dactyls won't be touching hot water because that would be tantamount to murdering his own kin and he, Homer, would be guilty after the fact, whatever that means, but to Homer it sounds scary enough.

Homer is confused. "But Uncle, don't we eat culls, me and ye?" Uncle reminds him that of course they do, but that's entirely different from dining on close kin and formerlies.

Abner drives Homer back to the dock and asks him to release Sonny. Homer lives at Uncle's house nearby and can walk home from the lobster pound. Not easily, perhaps, but he can make it. Abner then turns his truck around and drives off.

The crowd has dissipated leaving the aquarium standing alone on its stout socle illuminated by a dock light. The sign with Nietzsche's words is still there, a little older and shabbier and no doubt still ignored by passersby. Homer waits until the tail lights of Abner's truck disappear before saying, "I'm real sorry, Sonny."

"You ought to be more than sorry, peckerwood. You almost got me boiled alive. What the hell were you thinking? I come back to find out about Mutha and hear any other family news, and you treat me like a. . .*like a fucking lobster!*"

"Yeah, well, I'm real sorry. That's all I can do, is apologize. We figgah ye mutha's okay, but we don't get much news. I kin tell ye that Dobbin has bin all fixed. Tune-up and new paint. Found a junkyahd headlamp receptacle fah 'is busted one, and he tain't a padiddle no longah. Got the crease out'n the bumpah and smoothed it good. When ye sees 'is face he looks like a reg'lah, uh, a reg'lah tractah. He seems to love a'pullin' the caht with the bait and pots. I reckon that be all the family news." Many years ago some dolt operating a hay bailer had smacked Dobbin in the face and twisted the left tip of his front bumper into the hint of an incipient grin, a Mona Lisa smile etched in rusting metal. With this and his many joints and struts, widely spread appendages, and headlamps like goggled eyes, Dobbin had assumed the appearance of a lovable cartoon arthropod or over-size windup toy.

Sonny is still miffed. "That sign welcoming me home is ridiculous. I almost didn't understand it."

"Tain't no accident. Uncle made that sign hisself. The family don't write good, and we spell wusah."

"You're a dumb shit, Homer, but still kin. Now, will you please, *please* drop me off the dock?"

21.

ANOTHER AUTUMN, AND SONNY decides to take a road trip to end all road trips. Perhaps he's feeling what German zoologists call *zugunruhe*, the antsy ancestral urge to migrate. To reach his destination he must travel eastward starting from the vicinity of Suramoh Island and traverse the width of the Gulf of Maine to Georges Bank one hundred-eighty miles from the Maine coast. He will cross the Bank and at its eastern end follow the continental slope, which descends to the Atlantic abyss. There he will stay the winter, perhaps longer, seasons not meaning much several miles below the surface.

The trek begins through a seascape of Paleozoic geology. He treks along shallow, jagged gulleys perpendicular to the shore where the tides are irrigated by flooded rivers and levitate on rumors of seafoam. Overhead, a murmuration of pilchards attacked by seabirds shatters the spears of downwelling light. The gulleys dip into deepening channels that he follows east. He climbs up and down uncountable pinnacles, crosses ridges too numerous, narrow, and obscure to be satisfied with their station, coming to a place of couloirs where the granite faces of the cliffs bear wavy lines of schist, as if liquid smoke trapped and squeezed through tight crevices of raised bedrock had crystalized in sinusoidal waves. He tramps across submerged moraines and the same plains of gravels, cobbles, and boulders as before. Single-mindedly, he continues on, always east across the floor of the Gulf toward Georges Bank where twenty thousand years ago the weight of ten thousand feet of ice had compressed the bedrock and lowered the sea level by four hundred feet. And when the ice went away the sea returned, flooding the land, and the bedrock rebounded.

Two deep passageways run from the Gulf into the Atlantic: the Northeast Channel divides the northeastern end of Georges Bank from Browns Bank south of Nova Scotia; the Great South Channel separates Nantucket Shoals south of Cape Cod from the southwestern end of Georges Bank. Both provide access from the Gulf to the open Atlantic. The first, being directly opposite the Maine coast, is the closer and more logical route from Sonny's starting point to the continental shelf and the North Atlantic abyss beyond.

Sonny continues down the continental slope, for a time experiencing the warmer slope temperatures. Food becomes scarcer, the choices different. He might stop to crush and eat clams, detectable by the organic compounds pouring from their effluent siphons poking above the sandy sediment, and sometimes polychaetes wriggle into his path. He descends into the midnight zone, the constant darkness no more nor less an impediment than previously; he can navigate perfectly well using just the chemo- and mechanoreceptors of his numerous setae. Despite being deep below the surface, he remains unaffected by the enormous pressure. Unlike the lungs of air-breathing vertebrates and the gas-filled swimbladders of many fishes, all his tissues are fluid-filled and nearly

142

equal in density and compressibility to the surrounding seawater. For the same reason that makes his reception of the pressure component of sound unlikely, he can live comfortably at any depth.

He enters a field of immense boulders that rises abruptly like a mountain range, providing surface relief and permanent sediment-free places of anchorage for sessile organisms like sea anemones and other invertebrate homebodies. He probes around for edible items. Every crevice harbors aggregations seastars, mainly of the brittle and serpent species, crunchy but pretty much tasteless.

There are sponges, many of them unfamiliar. He pauses. Why not? A sponge itself has only moderate food value, but the tiny organisms packing its labyrinth of canals are certainly worthwhile, although only indirect access to them is possible. This means masticating and swallowing the sponges themselves. Well, here goes.

Sonny selects a specimen reported by the setae on his legs to be emitting a goodly amount of ammonia, a breakdown product of proteins. It seems promising. He snips off a chunk with his cutter claw and is not disappointed: good tastes and smells ooze out. He straddles the macerated mess he's just made and lets the pincers of his first two pairs of walking legs go to work autonomously selecting bits of what they assess to be edible and stuffing them into his mouthparts. He feels these miniature scissors underneath him snipping and picking. Nothing else is on the agenda except remain in place, masticate, swallow, grind the pulpy mess in his gastric mill, burp it up, masticate and grind again, repeat as necessary.

As he stands there in bovine stupor, grazing and swallowing, regurgitating and swallowing, a strange torpor sweeps over him, a weightlessness and sense of disembodiment as if at any moment he might rise into the water column and float off. The sensation is pleasant, relaxing, and vaguely unnerving. He steps away and begins seeking a shelter. He's stumbling, tripping, bumping into rocks despite being aware of their locations. Finally, he finds a crevice and crawls in. Sonny is stoned. These sponges or possibly their symbionts contain hallucinogenic marine tryptamines.

In the deep sea Sonny isn't aware of the cold so much as the experience of it. There is no shivering, no particular discomfort; rather, he adjusts to an overall slowing of the metabolic processes, becomes inured to the plodding pace of life. Throttle down and live longer. For what?

"Wake up, Sonny! Goddammit, wake up!" He's being shaken violently.

"Oh, it's you."

"Yeah, who'd youse think it was, dipshit, the fairy godmother?"

"I dunno. Nobody. I think I'm dreaming."

"Could be, but wake up and talk to me. Oy, you're stoned. How'd youse manage that down here on the, uh, the contin. . . ."

"Continental slope."

"Right. Christ, Hell must be like this place. Totally dark, I mean, except fer the fires. So where are they?

"What?"

"The fires. Holy shit! Did youse just feel a tremor?

"Of course. Minor seaquake. You feel them a lot around here so close to the bedrock Dude, we're like, deep." Sonny is coming around, sort of. He realizes he needs to get the conversation going.

"Hey Day Tripper! How're your swimmerets hanging? Give me a meral spread, dude!"

"Hanging tough, Thunder Claw!"

Having a nickname is so cool, him a lifelong nerd, freak, outsider. . .finally in a place with occasional com-radery, rare though it is, where he basically looks and acts like everyone else; that is, his new conspecifics. Screw the human race. He, Day Tripper, and the Professor have become members of the species *Homarus americanus*, and among their kind nobody especially takes notice of individual appearances.

He and Day Tripper approach and give each other a meral spread, the gesture invisible in that blackness. It scarcely matters: between them it's deployed obversely as an ironic greeting between iconoclasts instead of a semaphoric threat. They touch crusher claws in the lob-ster equivalent of a fist-bump. Sonny says, "Where've you been? Haven't seen you around, what, in months? Years? Thought maybe you 'ate the bait.'" It's an expression occasionally used among formerlies, at least those still able to find humor in their situation. It refers to the act of stupidly entering a lobster trap enticed by the odor of rotten bait, something only a dimwitted homie would do.

"Been road-tripping, man, and somehow ended up here. Dunno why. Thought I might go south to warmer waters come winter, so in late summer I hiked south to Long Island Sound. Passed Sheepshead Bay in Brooklyn, the old fishing grounds, when, y'know, I usta fish, like, from a boat wit a pole? I told youse the story, remember? Been several years now, can't recall how many.

"Anyhow, it goes like this. It's a Friday and the next day is my birthday. My three best life-time buddies from kindergarten through high school take me to dinner at this seafood restaurant. We start in the bar at happy hour, suck-ing down the two-fer-one drinks, cracking wise, busting balls, how guys generally behave when out on the town. These is the schmucks who give me the name Day Tripper 'cause once on the party boat outta Sheepshead Bay I get loaded and puke over the railing. One of the crew points at me and says, 'Day Tripper,' meaning not a real sailor. My good buddies, my pals, is the ones who seen that the name sticks wit everybody in Brooklyn, the bastids.

"Anyhow, happy hour comes and goes. We decide to splurge and treat ourself to lobster. We're pretty sloshed. The waiter leads us to the lobster tank and says to pick our dinners. It's my birthday, right? Or almost my birthday. Close enough. So, I pick the biggest fucking lobster of the bunch. It probably weighs six pounds. The waiter says they sell lobsters by the pound, and I'm likely staring at a hunnert-clam main course. I say I don't care, that's my lobster, that's my big boy. We tell the waiter to call us when dinner is served and return to the bar. For some reason I get this hair across my ass that I feel sorry fer the lobster. I mean, it's gonna to be boiled alive and all. I go look at it again and see it waving its feelers. It's scrabbling at the glass wit some of its li'l feet and working its mouth really fast, like it has a toothache, and I'm thinking I can hear it say, 'Please don't choose me!'

"I wave the waiter over and tell him I'm changing my order to lobster carryout. 'I still want this one,' I say, and point to it, 'but it needs to be alive when I leave.' He nods. Nothing shakes Brooklyn waiters. They seen it all. I slip the guy a fiver and go back to the bar. A few minutes later he's at my elbow wit the lobster in a bucket of seawater. Not long after, we're seated at our table drunk as parish priests, me wit the bucket at my feet. While the other guys is cracking shells and drooling butter on their bibs I'm scarfing a cheeseburger and bending down now and then to look at my lobster and deciding I ought to let him go. I mean, what the hell am I gonna do wit a fucking lobster in a bucket? Think Maureen will be pleased? We don't even have an aquarium, fer chrissakes.

"Next morning is Saturday, my birthday. The celebration the night before was fer practice. We wake up in Jamie's pad when his alarm goes off at six ayem. Jamie's in his bed, I'm sleeping on the floor, Eddie's hogging the couch, Frankie is crashed in the armchair. We're suffering big-time wit major-league hangovers but bogarting prepaid reservations to go fishing on a party boat outta Sheepshead Bay. Can't waste that bread. We rally. The four of us start drinking beer and passing the bottle of bourbon soon's we're on deck, even before leaving the dock. By early afternoon we're toasted again, and my so-called buddies, my life-long pals, think it might be great fun to toss 'birthday boy' overboard in his birthday suit, which they do, then empty the bucket wit the lobster on my head when I surface. But down I go again, and the second time I don't come up. Instead, I'm sinking to the bottom changed into a lobster, the same one, I figure. Like, I'm now him and he's me and we're both one and the same, or something equally fucked up. I realize I should've eaten him and maybe saved myself the meta-, uh meta-. . . ."

"Metamorphosis."

"Oy yeah, thanks, buddy. Naturally, my body — I should say former body — is never recovered. Funny part? I miss out on attending my own wake beside the empty casket and seeing Maureen cry her pretty blue eyes out while her mother pats her and says over and over, 'Well, honey, I told youse so, but when did youse ever listen to my advice? Now, I ain't gonna say out loud I guaranteed something like this might happen when youse marry a turd like him, but better believe I'm thinking it.'

"Anyhow, while on this road trip I trudge near the scene of the crime, so to speak, and I got to admit it makes me a little sad. I wonder what the guys is doing to kill time and maybe stay straight, if they meet girls and get married, and such like that, and I might even have shed a tear or two fer myself and Maureen, who's no doubt remarried after finding another stiff wit steady employment, but when youse cry underwater who can tell? I walk around seeing other lobsters. No high-fives from the homies, but a lotta quick meral spreads flashed my way. You know New Yorkers and their attitude. Well, New Yorker lobsters ain't any different. Everybody seems in a big goddamn hurry, and no one stops to say hiyah, how ya doin'. It's like they're hustling off to catch the subway, meet gals or pals fer happy hour, get to Mass. . .something like that. Spent a few days under the Guinea Gangplank, just fer laughs."

"Under the *what*?" Sonny still feels woozy.

"You know, the Verrazano-Narrows Bridge. That's what New Yorker's call it. Anyhow, some strange stuff happens down there: trash of all kinds rolling through the strait, huge sharks drifting like submarines, ankle bones of mafia wiseguys sticking up from buckets of cement, and fierce currents. Very fierce currents. The place is invigorating, sort of a Coney Island under the sea, if youse catch my drift. So, I dawdle along in no hurry, setting up temporary shelters along the route and getting laid, same ol' same ol'. Nowhere in lobsterland do the homie chicks speak good English. In fact, they don't speak at all, they only buzz, but who cares?

"I finally slog clear to the western end of the Sound right outside the Big Apple itself, and whaddaya know, sick lobsters everywhere. Hunnerts of 'em, glassy-eyed and dopey wit shells like a bad case of acne. I bump into a formerly who tells me most of the citizens has caught lobster shell disease, but the locals got their own name fer it. They call it' lobster leprosy.' This formerly, he's got it too and figures he'll soon be worm food. Ugly situation, man. I get to thinking it could be contagious, y'know? I'm scared to eat the food and breathe the water, so I haul ass back to the Gulf of Maine where it ain't exactly vacation heaven but definitely healthier. Ain't seen a single case of that leprosy since I come back. From here on I'm hanging around, and if I feel an urge to grow and need to molt, or if I start packing around too many of them whatchamacallits and have to dump this shell, uh, them epi-. . . ." He taps his cephalothorax with a walking leg, trying futilely to remember the term.

"Epibionts."

"That's right. I'll move nearer the coast fer the warmer months, chow down and get fat, and then molt. I *hate* molting, really fucking hate it. Worries me shit-less. A guy could die molting. . .but hell, *c'est la vie* or whatever it is the wops say. Gotta keep the ol' shell clean and the powder dry, right? I pick 'em off whenever I can, them little epi-thingies, the bastids, but youse can't never reach that place in the middle of the back between where the shoulder blades usta be. The uh, uh. . . ."

"Areola."

"That's it exactly! How do youse remember this stuff? Oy, great bumping antennae witchu, but I gotta split. Hot little number waiting in a pile of boulders where I been crashing. This baby is a chix. A chicken lobster, get it? Ha, ha! I once had a human girlfriend who was double-jointed, but this one's hepta-jointed times ten.

Wit any luck she's newly molted and pliable. Let's me and youse hook up some night soon — or daytime, don't make no difference around here — hoist a few stars and squirts, maybe get high on whatever it was you ate. I'm inna book, as they say. I'll have my gal call your gal! Don't take no driftwood nickels, bro. Ciao."

Sonny is now straight, more or less, and about to remind Day Tripper that he isn't in the Gulf of Maine, but a long, long way from there. It doesn't matter. The whole episode has been a dream.

22.

THERE'S A TIME WHEN the light hurts but the dark wounds. When darkness creeps up like a vengeful snake, turgescent and eyeless yet staring. When it makes you want to hold onto yourself forgetting guile and subservience, dominance and the repatriation of quietude. Is it possible to multiply yourself out of this mess without being a gamete? Sad or not, with smallness comes sameness. It's possible to shrink individuality to invisibility and beyond, eventually losing it. Truly, the smaller the package the proportionately greater becomes the loss of self until finally everything is the same. Can two hydrogen atoms be told apart? Two electrons? That's life at scale; size matters. Whatever size you are, that's you.

His days and nights are somber, barely episodic. He envies the ordinary, those times as a human when he despaired of emotions, wishing to be an uncaring bundle of animal instincts reacting mindlessly. He's passing through a place on the seafloor of unusual calmness, although not really: nature can never be motionless, only seemingly in repose. Molecules everywhere are jumping, combining, separating as if taking joy in effervescence. Experiences aren't in short supply. Ennui is the issue. He's seen death, not knowing its name is entropy. He's yearned for a sign of paltry human frailty, a hiccup, a fart, a stubbed toe, anything.

He remembers recently passing through the twilight zone where dull gray had sopped up the horizontal background, and how on entering the midnight zone the gray disappeared, swallowed by a stygian black of impossible density. It seems almost liquid, an atrament of sorts. It had bounded up the slope in eager swirls dissolving the gray in its path, engulfing it completely as a black hole imbibes light. If so, how is this possible? Where does the gray water go when the black water consumes it? Can a liquid dissolve in another liquid? Isn't dissolution the process by which a solute vanishes in a solvent? Not always. One liquid can dissolve in another if their polarities are similar, but Sonny doesn't know this and for some reason finds the issue strangely vitiating. Perhaps the Professor could have explained it to him. However, at the moment this is Sonny's narrative, and he isn't thinking clearly. How can the depth possibly rise toward him? If depth is a continuum then every level should be in equipoise even in its infinite divisions, each nailed neatly in place. Or so it seems, assuming Sonny has even thought through matters this far.

Poke past it, he tells himself. It's only blackness, a noncolor, the same as no color, and anyhow you're colorblind. Look around. Say, is that even possible, looking around? No, you might as well be completely blind. Use those antennae like white canes, just keep tappin' along. You'll eventually get. . .somewhere. No matter, you brought this on yourself, silly lobster! You asked for a time-out at a location of near-sensory deprivation, and now you have it. Systems check: dashboard lights blinking for the other neurosensors. Chemoreceptors still

useful even if input data are monotonous; smells con-
solidated and generally stale. Mechanoreceptors mostly
on standby. Hardly any current to detect and orient to;
few vibrations worth sorting. Coordinates? One direction
pretty much the same as another making compass roses
superfluous. Segueing into that floral thought, if meeting
a lady lobster down here anxious to molt, give her a big
bouquet of anemones, the sea-dwelling kind.

Here in the midnight zone light indeed has van-
ished, and after several more days of steady descent he
emerges onto the level abyssal plain, disappointed that it
seems like a garbage dump, a rubbish heap, a *décharge*,
the basin of the oceanic cesspool. Everything tastes
and smells like the sediment, which consists largely of
decomposing marine snow that rains down endlessly
from the upper zones, tiny aggregations of bacteria and
particulate matter comprising dead plankton and zooplankton pellets. Its binding agents are microscopic
shreds of disintegrating salps and the macerated mucus
of sea jellies, ctenophores, and shed by swimming fishes.
Digested then digested again, enveloped and dissolved
and reconfigured during miles of sinking from the eutro-
phic and twilight zones all the way to the seafloor.

A great whale has died and come to rest on the
bottom, its form a self-defining tumulus giving transient surface relief to the otherwise featureless plain.
Predators are gathering to prey on one another and on
scavengers attracted to the carcass. Suspension feeders
arrive as drifting larvae and attach to its surfaces; microorganisms stake claims in preparation to soak up the
liquid residues of decay. An enthusiastic conurbation of
unlikely outliers has crossed the abyssal desert for such
a rare feast, which in the near-frozen surroundings will

continue for years. They feed silently in each other's mindless company, unwitting companions in this obscure symposium on symbiosis, unsuspecting worshippers of impromptu death.

He has yet to encounter another lobster, but is not surprised. The abyssal benthos is immense, the life harsher than in the upper, more salubrious zones. Many of the lobsters that live permanently in the abyss or visit regularly are large. Of the true giants found at any depth, most are males. In these monsters the combined weight of the claws is two-thirds the total weight.

Sonny has not molted in several years, and his carapace has become rough and scorious, overgrown by epibionts representing several phylogenetic nations. He shifts and flails like a bongo drummer, inducing in the near vicinity piquant particle displacement and rampant vibrational unholiness. He has traipsed to these new latitudes seeking the enlightenment of added buoyancy. Here, within deep basins, the coldest water has slunk, burdened by the agony of its higher salinity. This place has never known daylight. It sulks in black silence. The currents have slowed nearly to a stop, and the monotonous seafloor is blanketed by fine sediment that when stirred has the same slow settling velocity as dust motes in an airless room. He knows he should return to the shallows and molt, but his exoskeleton still fits comfortably, and now at twenty-five or so pounds the notion of once again competing for dominance seems ridiculous. There's no one to bother him. The Professor is right to think of retiring here despite the shitty climate and general absence of delectable viands and other amenities.

Since migrating to the abyss he's had sex just once. . . . Truthfully, almost once. Not unusual. The icy environment, unlike the shallow warmth of the euphotic zone, is not conducive to molting and reproduction. His partner during that single attempted tryst had been a strange formerly, a premolt atavistic hippy of a lobster visiting the abyss mostly to trip on the sponges. Paradoxically, she hoped never to molt again, making her appearance at his shelter puzzling. Communication had been an issue, and in the end their coupling failed.

She had blundered into him trailing raiments of sea anemone tentacles and the feathery feet of barnacles; from within the confines of their aragonite calyces a cluster cold-water corals cemented to her carapace shuddered in unison. These and their associate epibionts weren't just fashion statements, they were her "friends" (she said), and they were "thrilled" (she claimed) to be chauffeured across the seafloor instead of stuck permanently to boulders with a view that never changes. Never mind that none of these camp followers possessed eyes with which to enjoy the view, or that it was even visible in the blackness. To keep them with her she had vowed never to shed her shell. One way of succeeding had been by moving to the icy deep where her growth would be slowed.

No trawls to avoid these miles down. Too inhospitable for gods, ghouls, or ghosts, for omens good and bad. Yahweh doesn't visit to nod approvingly at the sweet scent of the sacrificial lamb's burning fat splattered against the altar. He's spreading his fury elsewhere; the unctuous should try a Middle Eastern desert and abandon this one. Absent too are giant predators bristling with external taste buds and empty saucered eyes. Silenced are canted chirps of the supercilious, the stolid, the superstitious.

Here, the blind must create memories and the

images to inhabit them from senses other than sight. Here, all are functionally sightless, and despite its vast emptiness the abyss lacks space to sequester remembrance. He tries picturing the sun, but feels only a stirring that passes through him quickly as a neutron. Irrelevant thoughts gestate to term, are born as boredom. Strange, he thinks, to smell and taste but not salivate. But what purpose would saliva serve? Moisture is hardly in short supply. Saliva is obviously useful to land-dwellers who abandoned aquatic life and embraced desiccation. Why must I crawl, he asks himself, when for a couple of weeks as a larva I could fly among fellow plankters under the sun's warmth? I experienced that, but retain no recollection of it. When I transitioned it was as an adult lobster. Would grieving a lost larvahood be proper, even if just one individual in fifteen thousand survives from hatching to breeding age?

It's dark, you say? What can we know of this vanta-black substance that permits no invasion or erasure? Hello Houston, abyss to base! We can't see jack-shit, as in I don't have to reach out to touch the darkness, it's on and in me. It's *become* me, or I've become it, whichever. I'm invisible. It's like being lost in space. Basically, *there's no light down here*. The unnamed are everywhere: what's that, who's what? Hey you, microorganisms able to break down chitin and dissolve me away! Anybody there? Good god, I seem to be standing in them knee-deep, but which knees and how many? No stopping here, Lobster-Buoy, nossir, you'll be engulfed by that soft microbiotic mouth, swallowed, digested, shat out. Relax. It chews patiently, soundlessly. Best move on. . .somewhere.

At the bottom of a deep rift his temperature sensors detect heat. The near-freezing water has become perceptibly warmer. Vision is useless in this perpetual night, but the seawater now smells and tastes strongly of sulfur and iron. He can only sense part of it, but before him is a towering chimney of precipitates formed from a hot slurry of mineral-rich water spewed continuously through an opening in Earth's crust. He tap-taps its base with his second antennae and finds that life is flourishing. These deep-sea vents are oases of energy in the otherwise impoverished surroundings. Photosynthetic production in the euphotic zone, impossible in the absence of light, has been supplanted down here by chemosynthesis, a specialty of certain bacteria and other microorganisms.

He trembles in the sea's ineffable sighs, smells and respires its throbbing economy, touches the contours of its vengeance; he wallows in its deflected fault lines, its quivering instance of immortality. Patient voices cascade to him from upper ecological zones. They speak in strange accents and hum appeasing stories. Distracted, he stumbles against another deep-sea vent, comforted by the warm rain of its heat-laced plume, pausing to dream in chemically reduced sulfuric bliss.

Snap to. He keeps moving, headed nowhere in particular. While ambling along some days, weeks, months later he suddenly senses a presence. A very large animal nearby is breathing, and in the still surroundings its exhalations are generating substantial turbulence. He take a few slow steps and blunders into the beast. Has this been a fatal mistake? Sonny is a big lobster, but this creature, whatever it might be, is massive. Retaliation could be imminent. Sonny is unsure what to do. Stand his ground? Back-flip away? Terrified, he does nothing. An antenna from high overhead brushes one of his second antennae. Another lobster, obviously, but how could this be? It towers over him. Oddly, there's no blast of piss in his face, no demanding a meral spread, but then what would be the point? Anyway, he hasn't entered the other lobster's shelter. There's nothing here but an empty plain. They touch antennae again, and Sonny tentatively begins a haptic exploration. The other lobster stands stoically without protest. When Sonny has finished the other speaks hesitantly as if unsure of the words. In a low rumble he says: "I. . .am. . .Zarathustra. . . .Who. . .are. . .you?"

Sonny's examination has revealed that Zarathustra must weigh a hundred pounds, maybe more, and his claws seem big enough to pulverize granite cobbles into rock dust. Each weighs at least thirty pounds, more than Sonny's entire body.

Zarathustra says, "You. . .may. . .join. . .me. . .if. . .you like."

Sonny eagerly accepts the offer. He thanks Zarathustra and asks where he's going. As Sonny is to learn, Zarathustra, having not thought much in human language for quite some time, occasionally lapses into stream-of-consciousness anacoluthons that seem directed at no one. He says, "I. . .am. . .going. . .to. . .a place. . .of. . .the. . .day before."

As he and Sonny slog through the powdery sediment, he mutters, "I. . .was here. . .once again. . .before now." Sonny is reminded about what the professor once said, that ignorance of language eventually devolves into a language of ignorance. Having had few opportunities for dialogue over many years, Zarathustra has lost much of his capacity for making his words understandable. If his solitary, nomadic life continues unchanged, someday his vocalizations will consist entirely of buzzes even in the presence of other formerlies. Maybe what he needs, Sonny thinks, is the mental stimulation of conversation. This proves true, and Zarathustra's fluency improves as their time together stretches out.

Sonny eventually asks him what he remembers of his youth. Zarathustra seems puzzled, perhaps suffering a flash of anomia. After several minutes of silence he speaks haltingly, as if still uneasy about stringing words together in coherent sentences. He remembers being frail and clumsy as a youth, barely able to walk or even to stand, as if an unseen force was relentlessly dragging him to the ground and punishing him for his very efforts. He felt at peace only when immersed in enough water to float, which alleviated the effect of this force, leading him to think he might be more at home in the ocean than on land.

His mutha owned a failing farm on a hilltop in Downeast Maine, and at the bottom of the hill was a tide-pool. He would limp and crawl down there to immerse himself and look at the stars and the moon. His eyesight, he tells Sonny, was terrible even then. He says that he can no longer remember the purpose of the stars and asks if the moon is still there.

Sonny assures him it is, and that the stars continue to hover at their fixed coordinates without any purpose; they simply exist. Zarathustra flicks his second antennae in acknowledgment and continues.

He recalls a summer night when the incoming tide brought a lobster into his pool. It was male and unusually large, and its presence had a calming effect. As a coastal Mainer he had been around lobsters all his life, not thinking much about them until that moment. He explains that in those times lobsters were used as fish bait and fertilizer and sometimes fed to prisoners. No

one purposely fished them. Humans living in eigh-
teenth-century New England considered lobsters an
inferior food and generally overlooked them despite
their ready availability. Many would wash ashore after
storms and could be plucked easily from the tidal wrack
even by children, although simply leaving them for the
gulls and to rot was more common.

Anyway, he continues, this particular lobster could
have gone back to sea with the turning tide, but chose
instead to remain. Through the night the two did little
but stare at each other. When the eastern sky predicted
dawn he rose to leave, but the lobster clutched at him
gently and tugged at his spindly legs as if imploring him
to stay. He couldn't, of course. His mutha would be waiting, and he had chores. Moreover, sunlight is unbearably
blinding to lobsters, as it also was to him back then. He
counted on the eternal dimness of the farmhouse with its
shuttered windows and absence of candles. Reluctantly,
he left the tidepool, climbed laboriously up the hill, and
recounted this experience to his mutha. She warned him
to be careful, that certain lobsters can be very persuasive
and trick young men into abandoning the land for an
uncertain life under the sea.

Zarathustra pauses his story, as if trying to gather
certain thoughts and events stored away or perhaps even
banished many years before. He tells Sonny that he was a
weakling as a youth, unfit for many undertakings, including
soldiering. The American colonies had begun a war with
the Redcoat regulars, the army of a kingdom across the
Atlantic whose ruler intended to keep them subjugated.
But many in Maine and elsewhere in the colonies wanted
to be independent, and so they fought for this right.

He remembers a sea battle called the Battle of

Machias, a village near his mutha's farm on the Downeast coast. The king's sailors were defeated. There was much celebrating, and afterward privateers continued to harass the foreign fleet until the end of the revolution, which the Americans won.

He had visited the tidepool intermittently throughout the conflict hoping to meet the lobster again. Even on winter nights when ice tessellated the rocks he crept down the steep hill and immersed himself, but the lobster never appeared. Then on a balmy summer night as he lay soaking in a rising tide his lobster washed in on the flood. The moon was full, and despite being sight-limited he was immediately recognizable. They stared at each other until the tide reversed and they were swept without his protest into the sea together. Zarathustra pauses, then says, "I. . .became him. . .and he. . .became me. . . .We. . .became. . .one."

Sonny is astounded. He describes to Zarathustra how closely their life-stories match, then blurts telepathically that Zarathustra must be at least two-and-a-half centuries old. Zarathustra seems unimpressed, saying in words free of hesitation, "I was here once, except that was the day before."

The temperature is a degree or so above freezing, the current creeping over the substrate seems catatonic, almost indifferent. In these conditions they eat little, sometimes going days without food, lacking any inclination to forage. Because safety isn't a concern, they seldom seek shelter. Around them serried pinnacles of stone rise from the seafloor like the shrouded backs of goblins, obscure and silent. They stop a moment, and Zarathustra says, "There is no darkness darker than the darkness you don't see." Then he turns, and they trudge on.

Sonny dreams while on the move, images growing like epibolies over the surfaces of previous dreams, edges curling and centers siphoning away earlier superimpositions. Nothing has context; there is never a narrative. These waking dreams flip through his mind at the speed of movie film, pictures frozen in comically accelerated motion. Zarathustra says suddenly, "There is no cure for death. Life is only a fleeting remission." Social interaction has sharpened his language skills during the intervening months — or has it been years — but were these cryptic thoughts always present, fully formed and licking silently around the ragged edges of his solitude?

Zarathustra says, "The world above is topsy-turvy and sheds none of its life this deep." Is this gibberish, the muttering of a senile crustacean misusing words from years of monkish ascesis and isolation? Was "light" and not "life" what he meant? But suppose it had not been a mistake, a simple fumbling of language? Then speculation can include other possibilities. Although Zarathustra's statements — and they were always statements, never questions — occasionally came across as nonsensical or paradoxical, most hinted at a kernel of truth. These seemed similar to parables or koans, perhaps containing in their stringent paring a profound meaning. Did Zarathustra intend that Sonny decipher his words, pose questions prompted by them, request enlightenment as might a disciple? He concluded that the answer could be part or all of this, or none of it, still puzzled whether the incoherent mumblings and putative sage sayings were random sparks from a divided state or coruscations released from a sequestered inner universe of allusive wisdom.

On the assumption that indeed Zarathustra is the

apotheosis of lobsterhood and lacking another plan, Sonny decides to tag along as his acolyte, at least for a while. He will follow Zarathustra so long as he's tolerated. How long might this be? Who knows? Days perhaps, or centuries.

They proceed slowly in tandem, unafraid, Zarathustra always in the lead. A leader, Sonny thinks, on an endless sojourn with neither objective nor destination. When he brings up the possibility of a goal, hoping for a glimmer of purpose to their travels, Zarathustra says, "We are too much in the becoming to ever arrive." On they go, stopping for extended periods to forage around thermal vents where life throbs, food is plentiful, and their appetite returns. They sometimes linger for weeks, months, maybe years. The warm mineral waters stimulate growth, then rarely one or the other feels a tightness inside his chitinous armor and needs to molt. The other stands guard until his companion's shell hardens sufficiently to permit travel. Sonny is now sixty pounds, Zarathustra even more monstrous than when Sonny met him.

Sonny sometime experiences a fierce yearning for light. He considers that Zarathustra has persisted in the abyss perhaps a century or longer, but he is unique, invincible, and seemingly disregards most sensory stimuli, including the occasional signal from his gastric mill that he should eat. But how long, Sonny wonders, can he himself endure this world of debasing mental poverty where love songs and threats arrive as an amalgam of discordant crackles and grunts, low-frequency drummings and scrapings, where the eternal blackness envelops like a malevolent entity? In this place the dietary choices are so limited that scavenging has usurped predation, and reproduction is a memory. Maybe in time he'll become oblivious like Zarathustra, content simply to be in motion.

And time. Of what use is such an arbitrary notion other than separating day from night and partitioning the seasons? These invented dichotomies and false concatenations accumulate one atop the other until they begin to vanish beneath life's rubble. How many days, months, years? No one counts. Once again, lobsters don't track time. They live entirely in the present. Only the formerlies among them think backward and forward, but less often as the past slips from memory and the present fades to an unknowable future, which, through a trick of anamorphosis is again the present. Thus, even for formerlies time drifts by unnoticed until their lives, like those of ordinary lobsters, are absorbed by sensation. Then they become subservient to their receptor systems, regressing into packets of mindless salty solutions encased in chitin, superfluous tendrils of that vast mindless solution, the sea.

ACKNOWLEDGMENT

I'M GRATEFUL TO KENT Davis and Roy Manstan for comments and suggestions on parts of the manuscript.

www.ingramcontent.com/pod-product-compliance
Lightning Source LLC
Chambersburg PA
CBHW031237260626
47169CB00007B/2344